Martha
AND
THE Slave
Catchers

Martha

AND

Slave

THE

Catchers

HARRIET HYMAN
ALONSO

SEVEN STORIES

7

TRIANGLE
SQUARE
books for young readers

New York • Oakland • London

A SEVEN STORIES PRESS & TRIANGLE SQUARE
FIRST EDITION

Artwork by Elizabeth Zunon

SEVEN STORIES PRESS
140 Watts Street
New York, NY 10013
www.sevenstories.com

College professors and high school and middle
school teachers may order free examination
copies of Seven Stories Press titles.
To order, visit www.sevenstories.com
or send a fax on school letterhead to (212) 226-1411.

Library of Congress Cataloging-in-Publication Data

Names: Alonso, Harriet Hyman. | Zunon, Elizabeth, illustrator.
Title: Martha and the slave catchers / Harriet Hyman Alonso ; illustrated by
Elizabeth Zunon.
Description: New York : Seven Stories Press/Triangle Square, 2017. | Summary:
When the 1850 Fugitive Slave Law passes, thirteen-year-old Martha, the
daughter of abolitionists living in Connecticut, embarks on a journey of
self-discovery as she travels south to save her kidnapped adopted brother
Jake, the orphan of a runaway slave. | Includes bibliographical references.
Identifiers: LCCN 2017047841| ISBN 9781609808006 (hardback) |
ISBN 9781609808013 (ebook)
Subjects: | CYAC: Slavery--Fiction. | African Americans--Fiction. | Racially
mixed people--Fiction. | Abolitionists--Fiction. | Fugitive
slaves--Fiction. | Identity--Fiction. | United
States--History--1815-1861--Fiction. | BISAC: JUVENILE FICTION /
Historical / United States / Civil War Period (1850-1877). | JUVENILE
FICTION / Historical / United States / 19th Century. | JUVENILE FICTION /
Historical / United States / General.
Classification: LCC PZ7.1.A468 Mar 2017 | DDC [Fic]--dc23
LC record available at https://lccn.loc.gov/2017047841

Printed in the United States of America

2 4 6 8 9 7 5 3 1

For Joe

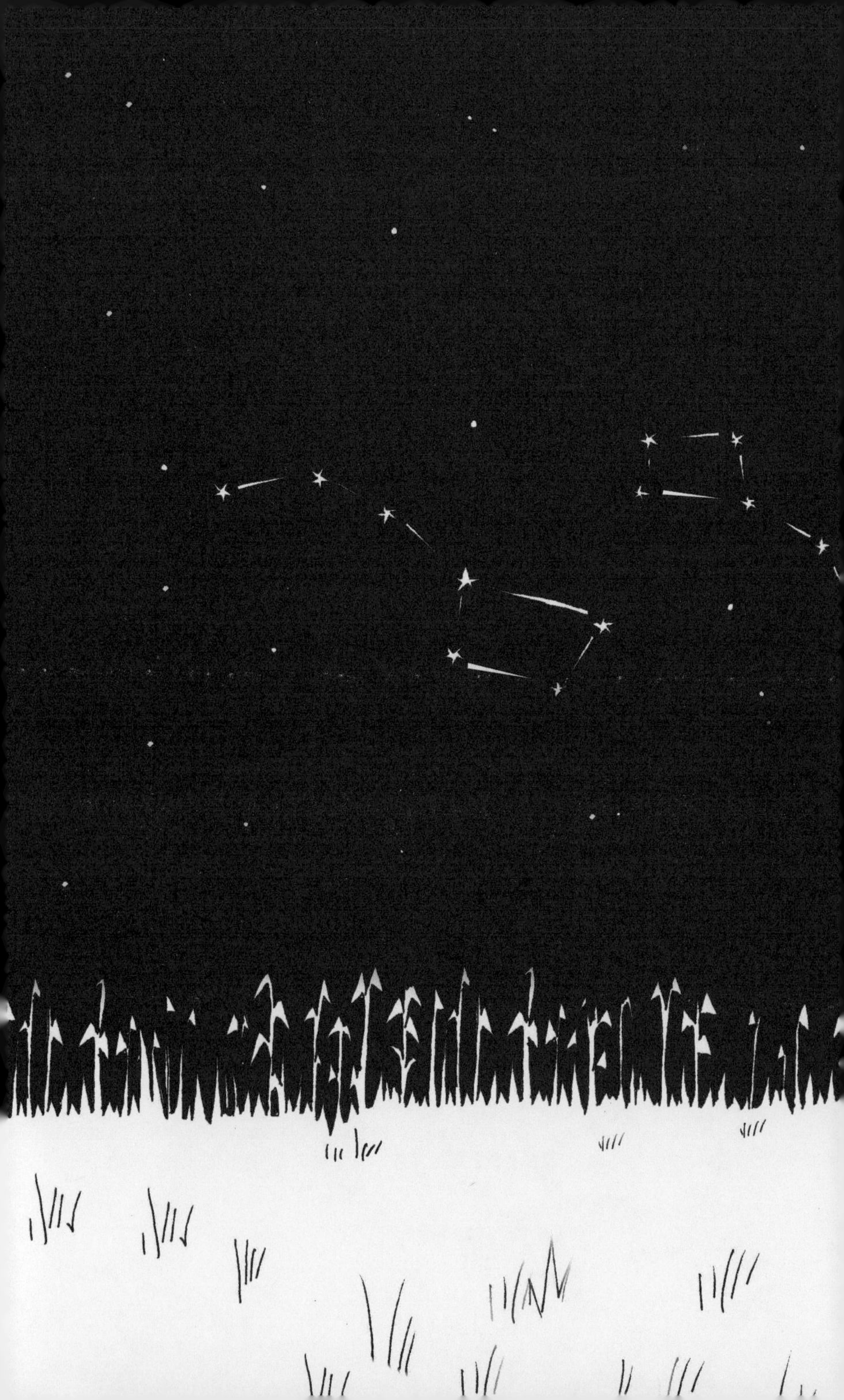

Contents

MARTHA BARTLETT jolted awake, her eyes wide open, her heart pounding so hard it hurt. She looked around the dimly lit room from the quilt cocoon that encircled her body on the plush, but simple, sofa. Someone had placed a soft pillow under her head, but she had no idea who. The room itself was unfamiliar. Its fireplace, brick walls, and rocking chair reminded her of home, but it was not her home. She knew that much at least, but not much more.

It was an effort to push the quilt away, but she longed to sit up. As she did, pain ripped through her arms, legs, and back. Gingerly, she touched her left eye, which throbbed in agony. Then she felt the bandage wrapped around her aching head. What had happened to her?

For several long minutes, she willed her brain to work. Think. Think harder. Try to remember. She closed her eyes tightly and opened them again, believing that perhaps the movement would spark a memory. In between two long blinks, she spotted a light blue square envelope with "Martha" printed in bold letters on the small table next to her. She knew that was her name, but still, she just stared at it. For some reason she did not understand, the letter's presence frightened her. Finally, though, she reached for it.

As her trembling hands touched the envelope's flap, she realized just how weak she was. Her finger could hardly work its way under the wax seal to break it. Then, she almost ripped the thin, fragile paper as she took the letter out and unfolded it.

She began reading.

4 July 1854

My dearest daughter,

Martha immediately recognized the handwriting. "Papa," she whispered, as the warmth of home reached out to her and, as if by magic, her papa's twinkling blue eyes smiled at her.

This letter comes to you through a trusted friend. I write it without knowing if you are safe, where exactly you are, or even being able to scribe your name or the name of the other I fret over.

The other. The fuzz in her head cleared slightly. Jake. She remembered her younger brother, Jake. Where was he? In a panic, Martha pushed herself to her feet. The room spun around and she promptly sat down, tilting her head forward onto her lap. As her dizziness eased, she saw an image of her and Jake running away from something bad. But what? She picked up the letter again, hoping it would give her the answer she needed.

Squinting to keep the print in focus, she read on:

As has been so for almost your entire thirteen-plus years, we live with secrets and lies, hiding the truth from a world racked with the abomination that is slavery. The result is before us now. Separation and hardship and who knows what else. It grieves me that I cannot be with you now to return you to your normal life. In truth, I do not know when that day will come, although I hope it will be soon. Currently, it is far too dangerous for you here at home. So, I have given our friends permission to take you to a safe place.

Rest assured, everyone here is toiling with all our might to rid the evil from this place. And we shall *succeed. I am sure of it.*

Martha's eyes welled up with tears. She had never been away from her parents before she left home just a few weeks ago. Why had she gone? She thought hard, but it was all a blank.

Your mama is not doing well.

Mama. Martha longed for her lovely mama, who had been ailing for several years. But from what?

Fear, worry, secrets, and lies have all lodged them-selves in her mind. Nowadays she does not move from her favorite rocking chair in the parlor. She only stares out into a world I am not a part of, mumbling in her Quaker Plain Speech about her childhood and the glories of her youth when nonviolence and goodwill encased all that she did. The morning you left, she went to your room and took your rag doll and now talks to it as if you were here. "Thee is a good girl." "Keep thy brother safe." "I love thee both."

Martha pounded on her head, then winced. What were these secrets and lies that had so hurt her mama that she had withdrawn from the world? Why couldn't she remember? Somewhere deep inside she knew her mama needed her and that she had to get home. Who would take care of her if she wasn't there?

B_____ comes over once a day to help tend to her. She takes our laundry and cleans the house as well. She has been a godsend considering all the responsibilities she has at home helping her own mama with the house and the many children. She sends her love and wishes you safekeeping until she can see you again.

Yes, of course. Becky, her best friend. She knew in her heart that she could rely upon her. Remembering Becky also brought back Caleb. Martha's mind drifted to the sense of him holding her and kissing her softly, but she forced her eyes to focus once again on her papa's words, words that were helping her mind to wake up. It was as if he was right there in the room with her, holding her hands, and urging her to come back to life.

The day you left, C_____ had a most terrible con-
frontation with his father. He discovered that it was
he who revealed our secret, all for a monetary reward.
C_____ says he will never be able to forgive him. He
packed his possessions, left home, and now stays in our
attic room. It is a great comfort to have him at my side
in the woodshop. Besides, there is so much work to do
that I would flounder without him. He is very regretful,
dear daughter, of his treatment of you. But I think what-
ever passed between you will have to be settled once you
return home. I sense from him that all will work itself out
once you see each other and speak deeply.

Martha ran her finger across the coded *C_____*
as if by doing so she could transport Caleb to her side.
She smiled as she felt in her pocket for the handkerchief with the embroidered red rose he had given her.
Rubbing it against her cheek brought him closer, but
she had no idea what they had quarreled about.

Martha drew in a deep breath. The oppressive heat
in the room added to her light-headedness. Sweat trick-
ling down her neck dampened the shirt she was wearing. She ran her hand under the collar to loosen it.
Why did she have on a boy's shirt? She gazed down at
her legs. And boys' pants? She instinctively reached
for one of her long plaits that she liked to twirl around
her finger. Nothing. Frantically, she dropped the letter and grabbed both sides of her head, feeling for her
cherished hair. Who would be so cruel as to cut it off?
Could her papa tell her? She picked up the letter once
again and anxiously looked for an answer.

You have been a brave and honest girl, my lovely one, and I pledge that I will do everything possible to bring you both home very soon. In the meantime, you must do all in your power to protect yourself and not to fret about us. I will anxiously await news from you, and I will send news back. Our friends will see to that.

As always, I remain your loving father.

Her papa said nothing more and apparently knew little of what had happened to her since she had left home. For now, she was on her own and desperate to pull her memories together, regain her equilibrium, and find out where she was and what had become of her brother. She folded the letter, kissed it, replaced it in its envelope, and put it into her pocket. Then exhaustion overtook her. Involuntarily, she leaned her head against the back of the sofa and closed her eyes. As she relaxed, scenes of her life in the small town of Liberty Falls, Connecticut, flooded her mind. And with them came memories of Jake.

JAKE ENTERED Martha's life when she was just six years old. Until then, she had been a happy-go-lucky little girl without a worry in the world. Her parents' love and care embraced her every day, and even her natural shyness often fell by the wayside as they shared their joy of life with her. October was her special month. The hot Connecticut summer was over, and in its place came cool, crisp days, fluffy white clouds, and the spectacular red, orange, and yellow autumn leaves that fell off the trees by the end of the month. Martha loved to jump into the huge mounds her papa raked just for her. She would then throw the colorful shapes up into the air with both arms swirling around to make leaf storms.

Best of all, Martha looked forward to the harvesting of the huge orange pumpkins that grew inch by inch all summer and early fall until even her strong papa could hardly lift them. She always laughed as he struggled and made loud groans.

"Mahthah, Mahthah," he would say in that New

England accent he told her came from growing up in Maine. "Help me!"

"Papa, I can't," she would respond, jumping up and down. "I'm too little."

"That may be so," he would answer. "But not for long."

Then he would wrestle the huge orange orbs into the wagon, saying, "This pumpkin weighs more than our barn."

And Martha would always giggle and say, "Papa, you're lying, and you told me never, ever to lie. That it is a bad thing to do."

"So it is, my wise daughter," he would answer as they headed home so her mama could use the fleshy pulp for pies, breads, and puddings.

Martha also loved picking apples off the trees in the family's small orchard. Her papa would lift her up so she could pick the biggest, reddest piece of fruit, which she ate right away, the juice dribbling down her chin. Life could not be better.

But October 1846 was different. Everything about it was wrong. Instead of the cool weather she looked forward to, the air was warm and muggy, and most of the leaves were still green or just turning brown when they fell like lead to the ground. In bleak fog or drizzle, she trudged the quarter mile to school until one day her papa took pity on her and started providing rides on horseback. With a sigh, Martha gazed around her world that had gone from beautiful blues, greens, reds, and yellows to browns and grays.

The evening of October 11 was even stranger than all the others, for although it was hot and humid, her mama was frantically building a huge fire in the parlor hearth while her papa created an enormous pile of logs. In between their hurried labor, each kept casting an eye on the dirt road leading from the main thoroughfare to their small farmhouse. After an hour of squirming and pulling at her dress trying to get some air, Martha took her angry stand, the one with her hands on her hips and her right foot tapping, and complained, "Why are you making a fire? It's so hot already!"

"Martha Bartlett, do not pout and ask questions right now," her mama panted as she hurried about. Martha could see perspiration streaming down her flushed red cheeks, flattening the blonde curls that usually crowded out from her lace cap onto her face. Her confusion grew stronger when her mama gave her an order that simply did not make sense. "Go bring in some more wood for me. Thee can carry the lighter pieces, canst thee? Meanwhile, I shall go fetch the boiling water. We shall need it soon."

"Why?" Martha queried in exasperation.

Her mama continued to rush about. "Not now, Martha. Just do what I ask of thee."

"But, Mama . . ."

"Go."

Martha looked at her papa for an answer, but he remained silent as he piled one log on top of another.

"Just do as your mama asks," he insisted. And so, shrugging her shoulders, she did.

Huffing and puffing, Martha lugged several cut-up tree branches into the parlor. After she dropped them with an exaggerated groan near the hearth, her mama instructed her to go upstairs to her room.

"But why, Mama? It's only seven o'clock."

"Because I said so, child. And," she added firmly, "close thy door and do not come out until morning. Look at some of thy books that bring thee so much pleasure, or play with thy doll."

Martha nodded but persisted in staring at the fire, the large kettle of boiling water, and her parents scurrying around and constantly glancing out the window.

"Go!" her parents commanded in unison.

Martha grudgingly took the lard-oil lamp her mama handed her and left the room. She had expected this evening to be like most others when, after her papa said goodnight to his last customer and closed up his wood-shop, she and her parents sat peacefully in the parlor. Her papa read aloud from his abolitionist newspaper, *The Liberator*, while her mama sewed or knitted and Martha played with her dolls or toys. Martha liked to hear her parents' conversations. Occasionally, she asked a question about what slavery was like or about the anti-slavery activists her parents spoke about with reverence, but most times, she just listened and learned.

Some evenings her papa put his own reading aside to entertain her with children's stories from *The Slave's Friend*. "Papa," she might urge, "read me the one about Joggy and Lorina." And he would read the next installment of the story of the two African children brought to New York on a slave ship and then saved by the captain and a kind lady.

But that October night, when everything seemed upside-down and no one wanted her around, she decided to pay particularly close attention to what her parents were saying and doing, even though that meant misbehaving by spying and eavesdropping. She just had to know what was going on.

Reluctantly, Martha climbed the steep, creaky wooden staircase up to her room on the second floor of the old house that her great-great grandparents had built. She had never met any of her ancestors, who had all died before she was born, but every time she climbed the stairs, she looked at their likenesses in the frames on the wall.

"Hello, grandfathers Isaac and Jacob," she would say, or "Hello, grandmothers Deborah and Leah." Talking always eased the somewhat difficult ascent for her short, chubby legs. Oh how she wished for the day she would be taller.

She reached her room and, by habit, paused to glance across the narrow landing at her parents' bedroom and then at the ladder leading up to a trapdoor to the attic. Martha hated to go up there. It was so cold in the winter, so hot in the summer. Even though her mama cleaned it every day or so, it always felt dusty to her.

Still, even at her young age, Martha understood the importance of that attic room, which on a regular basis hid a runaway slave for a day, sometimes two. The slaves appeared and disappeared very quickly on their hard journey from the South to the North, even as far as Canada. Martha's farm was just one stop on the Underground Railroad and her parents just one pair of "stationmasters" who received their "packages" before sending them "up the line" to the next "station."

Although Martha's papa and mama did not ask anything of her in this secret and dangerous work, she was perfectly aware of a refugee's presence every time the attic floorboards creaked. Sometimes, when she peeked out her door when no one was watching, she caught a glimpse of a scared-looking black person being hustled up the ladder or her mama carrying food on her way to check on them.

Martha was proud of being raised in an abolitionist home, but she was far too young to completely understand what the Underground Railroad was or how it worked. Her heart told her, though, that if her parents participated in it, then it must be a good thing—a brave thing. And she looked forward to the day when she would be old enough to help her parents free the slaves. But she also knew how important it was to keep the Underground Railroad a secret. That was the hard part because she was by nature curious and could not help asking questions.

That night, when Martha walked into her cozy room and quietly closed the heavy door, she was most careful to leave it open just a little crack. Since runaways usually came late at night when the house was dark and everyone in the surrounding area asleep, it made sense that some other major event was taking place. And she wanted to know what it was. She sat down on her narrow bed, the one that her papa had made just for her with his very own hands, but she was too restless to look at her books or play.

In the end, she got up, moved her child-sized cane chair close to the small window next to her chest of drawers, and climbed onto it. By standing on her tippy toes, she could just make out her family's fields, now dark and empty of the harvested corn, pumpkins, and vegetables. But try as she might, she could not twist her head enough to see the dirt road and front of the house where she had just heard the sound of horses' hooves and of wagon wheels pulling up to the door.

Martha clambered down from the chair, almost knocking it over, rushed to her door, and carefully peered out toward the downstairs entrance, which faced the steps. From the dark emerged her uncle Jonah and sixteen-year-old cousin Ned with a thin bent-over figure between them.

"Shut thy door, Martha," came her mama's voice. "Now!"

Martha jumped back from the door as if struck by lightning, still leaving that teeny crack open. She turned down her lamp so no one would spot her from the darkness of the hallway and remained absolutely quiet. Leaning with her ear pressed against the door-jamb, she heard her aunt Edith say, "Come quickly, Sarah. She's almost ready."

The furtive whispers downstairs increased Martha's curiosity. Cousin Ned had once shown her how they hid runaways in the false bottom of their hay wagon that was then covered with straw. He and Uncle Jonah traveled the fifteen miles from their home southwest of Liberty Falls to hers, delivered their "package," and immediately drove away into the night. Martha could not remember a time, however, when her papa's twin sister, her aunt Edith, accompanied them. And what was "she," whoever "she" was, almost ready for? Try as she might, Martha could not make out all the words the adults were saying.

". . . need . . . take her . . . attic . . . the slave catchers . . . on her trail . . ." whispered her papa.

". . . don't know . . . can make it, Micah," countered Aunt Edith.

". . . no choice . . . all of our safety . . . especially

hers . . . help your papa . . . take the lamps . . . attic trapdoor . . . carry . . . hot water. Meanwhile, your mama and your aunt . . . come right up."

The next thing Martha heard was the two men bumping into the dark walls as they jostled the poor groaning woman up the steep stairs. As they passed Martha's door, she peeked out and realized this was a girl, not a woman at all. She was tall and beautiful with long, wavy black hair and the palest skin Martha had ever seen, and she looked no older than her cousin Ned.

Martha was shocked by how ragged and dirty the girl's dress was. Her thin shoes had such big holes in them that they could hardly stay on her feet. Yet, she had a delicate red silk embroidered shawl around her shoulders that she gripped tightly across her chest in her clenched fingers. Martha wondered where she had obtained such a beautiful thing.

For a brief second the girl turned her head, her almond-shaped hazel eyes catching Martha's own brown ones gleaming from the shadows. She attempted a smile but instead grimaced as another wave of pain grabbed her and she knotted up her face and lowered her head. It was then, when Martha's papa and uncle shifted their positions, that she saw the girl's huge belly and immediately understood she was having a baby. But she could not figure out why she was here. Could white people be slaves?

The next moment, Martha's uncle hustled up the ladder. He placed his arms under the girl's armpits and lifted her straight up. Martha's papa quickly followed with his arms around her legs. They were both trying very hard not to jar her, causing her even more agony.

In the blink of an eye they were gone, with the other three hurrying after them.

For hours, days it seemed to Martha, she heard only sounds—creaking floorboards, groans, hustling feet, and whispering voices. Then one loud scream followed by silence.

Time stood still, and Martha could no longer contain her curiosity. She ran out of her room and toward the attic. As she neared the foot of the ladder, she heard the small, feeble cry of a baby and her mama's clear voice: "He is alive, but very tiny and weak. I do not know if he will survive."

"But this poor girl," Aunt Edith sighed. "What will we do with her body?"

Martha's papa offered in such a low voice that she could hardly hear him, "I have some coffins in the workshop. We can use one of them to take her over to the town cemetery and bury her there. But we must move quickly."

"It's too sad," Aunt Edith added. "We don't even have a name to place on her grave. She never said it, and none of us asked."

"Even if we knew," commented Uncle Jonah dryly, "we couldn't use it, for even that might give us and this poor baby away. What are we going to do with him?"

Martha's mama said softly, "We'll decide that later. First, we must wrap her body in a sheet. It pains me that we have no time to wash and prepare her properly for burial. Edith and I will just clean her up a bit while thee, Micah and Jonah, prepare the coffin. Meanwhile, Edith, we must also warm up some diluted milk and water. The babe is sure to wake up shortly."

Martha sprang into action. Scurrying back to her room, again leaving the door open just a crack, she jumped into bed and pulled her quilt up to her neck. She was very careful not to allow the soft material to cover her ears.

"Let's go," put in her papa, and down they came in a rush to get to the wood workshop behind the house. After a short while, the men returned.

"We've placed the coffin in the hay wagon. Let's hasten to secure her in it, so we can be off to the burial ground," her papa said.

Although they moved as quietly as possible, Martha heard the two strong but tired men carry the slave girl's body down the ladder and prepare to descend the stairs to the first floor.

"Micah," Martha heard her mama whisper, "be sure to say a few words over her grave and to pray for some minutes."

Right next to her door, her papa answered, "I shall do the best I can, Sarah, but time is short, and there's a storm brewing, one of those big ones from the South. The wind is picking up something fearsome. We need to dig the grave and disappear before daylight. It could take us a good four or five hours to finish up, and the morning light will come up long before six. Besides that, who knows when the rains will begin. For now, snuff out the candles, bank the fire, and darken the house."

"God be with you," put in Aunt Edith.

Martha heard the men quickly leave, then silence for several moments as the two women lingered on the stairwell right outside her door. She, meanwhile, pretended to be asleep, opening her mouth and letting out, perhaps a bit too loudly, her habitual brief snorts.

"Oh, my goodness, Edith," her mama whispered in a hoarse voice. "Martha's door has been open a crack. I hope the curious little thing did not witness all of this." Opening her eyes just a slit, Martha saw her peek in at her. "She seems sound asleep, but I worry."

"Don't think about it now, Sarah," Aunt Edith soothed her. "If she did see something, you'll find a way to explain it, I'm sure. You already know the little dear heart has seen runaways here, but she holds her tongue well."

Martha's chest swelled with pride as her mama responded, "Thee speaks true. She is a real blessing, my little Martha is. But, come, Edith. Let us clean up everything and put the house to sleep."

By this time, Martha was so exhausted that after grabbing hold of her rag doll she fell into a deep sleep. Hours later, she awoke startled as she heard the sound of horses galloping up the road to the farmhouse. It was already daylight, but the house was quiet. Outside there was a strong wind blowing and sheets of rain were pounding on the rooftop and against Martha's window-panes. While she struggled to untangle herself from her blankets, her mama rushed in holding a little bundle in the colorful shawl Martha recognized as the slave girl's.

"Martha, there are slave catchers rushing up our road. Do not ask questions now, but I need thee to hide this little baby. Put him in thy doll's cradle and pretend thee is rocking thy doll and singing to her."

"But, Mama," Martha asked, terrified by the request, "what if he cries?"

"He will not, for I have given him just a small amount of laudanum to keep him quiet."

Martha had heard her parents say that some run-aways did that so infants would not cry on the journey and expose them to recapture. But she also knew that laudanum was some kind of dangerous medicine. Her mama had some for emergencies, but she told Martha never, never to touch it because it could make someone sleep forever if they took too much. She sure hoped that would not happen to this very tiny infant.

Although her mama was in a hurry, the always-curious Martha could not help asking, "Is this a slave baby, Mama?"

"No. His mama was indeed a slave, but he was born here in a free state. So by our laws he is free. But I am afraid the slave catchers will see things in a different light. They will say he is a slave because his mama was one. But I will explain it all to thee later."

As she placed the baby in the little doll's cradle, she added, "Thy papa is out in the fields bringing the cows and sheep in before the storm gets worse, so I must face these evil men myself." She then left, softly closing the door behind her.

Martha sat down on the floor and looked at the sleeping newborn. He fascinated her, just like the baby calves she once saw in the barn. Or maybe the little chicks. But he was a human version, a doll-like person. No wonder her mama believed Martha's toy cradle was a good place to hide him.

Under the tiny knitted hat her mama had placed on his head, Martha could see black curly hair. She recognized the hat as her very own when she was a babe, and it made her feel a kinship with this little soul. His face, so tiny with a little snub nose, had long fuzzy sideburns on each side and even a little mustache that made Martha giggle. To her surprise, his skin was a very light tan, almost the same shade as her own. For a brief moment, he opened

his unfocused almond-shaped gray eyes half-way. Then he slowly lowered his lids and drifted back to sleep.

A loud banging on the front door quickly brought Martha out of her reverie. With a pounding heart, she muttered, "The slave catchers." She had never seen one, but she imagined them to be very tall, strong, and armed with guns. Would they hurt her mama?

"What is it that thee wants?" Martha heard her mama's stern New England voice ask.

"We're looking for a female runaway slave. Young. Pretty. Light skinned, and big with child. You seen or heard of her?"

Martha could not see these men, but their voices and unfamiliar accents sounded as frightening as she had imagined. To keep calm, she prayed hard that they would not enter the house.

While she held her breath and remained absolutely still, a strange noise reached her ears. Looking down into the cradle, she saw the baby's lips all puckered up and moving, sucking in air. What if those awful men downstairs heard him? Not knowing what to do, Martha stuck her pinky finger into his mouth. She then began rocking the cradle and humming in as soft and calming a way as she could. He quieted, happily sucked away, and sank into a deeper sleep. Martha dared not move her hand even though she felt like a huge squishy whirlpool was going to drag the whole thing further into his mouth and down his throat.

Downstairs Martha's mama coldly responded to the slave owners' henchmen, "I have not encountered such a woman. Now excuse me, I have work to do."

"Well," a deep voice threatened, "we know this is hostile territory to us hardworking slave catchers, ma'am, so we'll be watching. And we may very well be back after this storm blows over. Just to take a look around, you understand."

"And that is illegal here, and I shall call a constable." Martha jumped as she heard her mama slam the door.

"Good day to you, too," they laughed loudly as they galloped away, leaving their ugly spirit tossing about on the wind gusts.

As soon as the sound of their horses' hooves disappeared, Martha's mama rushed up the stairs and into her room. Martha smiled at her, and her mama gave a hearty laugh.

"Thee has saved the day, my darling Martha."

"But, Mama," Martha answered despondently, "you lied. You told those men you hadn't seen such a person. But *I* saw her." She pressed on although her mama had given her a look mixed with concern and aggravation, "Do people on the Underground Railroad have to lie? Because you told me never to say anything that's not true."

Martha's mama moved over to the window and gazed out, sorrow written all over her face.

"Thee speaks true, Martha. Lying is sinful. But sometimes we must do things to fight against an evil such as slavery. So, in this case—to save this child— I have lied," she answered. With that confession, she returned to the cradle and pulled Martha's pinky out of the baby's mouth, causing a loud pop. "Now, let us get this child some nourishment."

"What will happen to him, Mama?"

"Thee knows he is motherless, Martha. And thee can

see how tiny and helpless he is. How would thee feel if we kept him and raised him as thy brother?"

Martha jumped up and down with glee. "Oh, yes, please, Mama. It would be so nice to have a little brother."

Her mama smiled as she picked up the baby and cradled him lovingly in her arms.

"Yes, thy father and I agree. His skin is light enough to pass as thy brother and his hair is dark like thine as well. We shall just tell everyone that we agreed to raise him for our poor recently widowed cousin Nora in Torrington, who died in childbirth. What does thee think?"

Martha hesitated. "But you don't have a cousin Nora, do you, Mama?"

"No," she sighed as Martha caught her in another lie.

Feeling bad for her mama, Martha quickly added, "I think it's a wonderful idea, Mama. I've always wanted a brother. But what'll we call him?"

"Thy papa and I think we should call him Jacob after thy grandfather who passed away the year thee was born."

"Jacob," she whispered. "Jake or Jakey, maybe."

"But no one, Martha," she added, "no one, not even Jacob, must ever know the true story of what happened here tonight. Does thee understand?"

"Yes, Mama. But is *that* a lie, too?"

"It is not a lie if thee does not say anything. And it will be necessary to lie if it means keeping him with us and from those who would see him as a piece of property."

"Who's that?"

"Slave catchers and slave owners. This baby will grow into a fine young man. And fine young slaves can be sold for a good price."

Martha looked at the baby with tears in her eyes.

"Will he turn black, Mama? And then the slave catchers will come and take him?"

"No, Martha. Slaves are sometimes dark and sometimes light. It depends on their parents and grandparents and even further back. This boy and his mother obviously have many white ancestors. I doubt he will be much darker than he is now."

Martha was totally confused, but she did not know how to ask more questions. Maybe when she was older, she would be able to understand about skin color, but not now. So she simply said, "I understand, Mama."

Her mama rushed to change the subject. "Tomorrow, I will take the babe and go to stay with Aunt Edith and Uncle Jonah for a week or so. Thy father will tell his customers that I have gone to Torrington to tend to Nora's funeral. The town gossips will spread the word so that when I return home everyone will accept Jacob as Nora's orphan. Thee will stay here and help thy father as much as thee can. Yes?"

"Yes, Mama. But you'll come back soon, won't you?"

"As soon as things have quieted down. Now, get dressed. There is no school today because of the storm, but I will need thy help to pack and to take care of the child."

And so Martha got up, did her few morning chores, and helped her mama prepare for her journey. All the while she felt conflicted about everything that had happened. A baby, she thought, a little baby to love and be a sister to. But it was all a lie and that worried Martha. What would happen if one day one little lie escaped? Would others follow? And what then?

CHAPTER 3

MARTHA WANTED to be a good big sister, but she found it most difficult. And she wanted to love her little brother, but at times, she was not sure she could. The first few months Jake was in her life were tiring and confusing. He was such a small baby that every two hours he wailed, demanding to be fed, and he took up all her parents' spare time and attention so that Martha felt left out. She sought every way she could to insert herself into their daily routines, but usually that meant she was asked to help with this or that or told to play by herself. What she really wanted was for her mama and papa to play with *her* or relax by the parlor hearth like they used to.

One frigid January night when Jake cried incessantly, Martha, unable to sleep, got out of bed, wrapped her quilt around her, and dragged herself across the hallway to her parents' room. There was her papa, rocking Jake in his arms while he paced the floor. Martha was overcome by envy as Jake nestled his little head on *her* father's breast, uttered a sigh, and drifted off to sleep.

"Papa," she whispered, surprising him with her presence, "why does Jake cry so much? He's driving me mad!"

Her papa looked at her lovingly and, putting his one free arm around her shoulder, gently moved her out of his room and into her own. "Let's talk here so that your mama can catch up on her rest," he said.

In the bright moonlight streaming in through Martha's window, she could see the shadows and deep lines of weariness under her papa's eyes. Meanwhile, Jake slept restlessly in his arms, from time to time his little body shaking with a spasm.

Her papa sank onto Martha's soft feather bed, leaning his back against the headboard. She, in turn, climbed up and snuggled against him, pushing so that he had to adjust his position in order not to jostle the baby too much and wake him up.

Then he spoke. "He's such a small baby, Mahthah, that he can't eat a lot at one time. Even with Mary Rogers nursing him three times a day and the cow's milk we give him at other times, his stomach seems upset and he gets cramps."

"But why does he always cry so much at night?" she whimpered.

"I don't know. Your mama and I think maybe the cow's milk doesn't agree with him. So tomorrow I'll purchase a goat from Zach Freeman. We hope that'll help."

"Papa," Martha persisted, "why doesn't he get bigger? He seems almost the same size as when he arrived."

"Again, I don't know," he said. Martha wondered why her papa, who knew everything about everything, should all of a sudden know so little. "Maybe his mother didn't get enough nutritious food when Jake was growing inside her. Or maybe she was beaten. Or maybe the journey north hurt him. We'll never know."

For several minutes Martha and her papa rested in silence. Then she offered tentatively, "Papa, maybe we shouldn't have kept him. Can we return him?"

Her papa's eyes shone with surprise at her blatant honesty. "Return him to whom?" he asked.

"I don't know," she answered in a very small voice.

"He's alone in this world, Mahtah, and we've promised ourselves that we'll raise him, and . . ." he paused, "love him. Would you have us return him to a slave owner?"

"No, Papa," Martha mumbled. Ashamed, but persistent, she added, "But maybe some other nice abolitionist family would take him."

"Oh, Mahtah, poor child," he responded and then pulled her closer to him and gave her a little snuggle. "He'll get bigger soon, and then we'll all get some sleep. And . . . have some fun."

After some time, Martha and her papa drifted off to sleep, Jake resting peacefully in her papa's arms and Martha curled up against his chest. Every few minutes her papa snored, she snorted, and Jake sputtered, sucked, and sighed.

And, indeed, Jake did begin to grow. By the summer of his first year, he had turned into a smallish, crawling bundle of energy. But as he grew, Martha noticed that her mama, instead of relaxing, became very anxious. She tensed at every loud sound. Her hands shook a lot. But worst of all, she never wanted to leave the farm, not even to go to the shops in town or to Sunday Quaker meeting. Martha missed her mama's former energy and enthusiasm for life and privately blamed it on Jake and the lie his presence had forced upon her family.

Martha's assigned job was to keep an eye on Jake so he would not get too close to the hearth fire or the well or traipse through the manure in the farmyard, or get into trouble in any number of other ways. Hands on her hips and foot tapping, she ordered him to behave. He rarely listened. Martha hated having to follow him around, even though at times she had to admit that Jake was a lot of fun. Martha could easily get him to laugh by making faces at him, wiggling her fingers, or tickling him under his arms. Because he was small, she could even pick him up and twirl him around, although her mama discouraged such rough play.

"Martha," her usually soft-spoken mama would nearly shout, "put him down. Thee will do him harm."

Martha always did as she was told, but at seven, she grew to resent having to spend so much time helping to tend to Jake. After all, she still had to feed the chickens, bring water in from the well, help clean the house, and assist in small ways with the cooking. She wanted to have some free time to make friends or to practice reading and writing, which she was just learning in school.

"Mama," she asked more than a few times, "may we go into town this Saturday and walk around and introduce Jake to folk?"

"Maybe another time, Martha," she repeated over and over again. "Jake is still so young that we do not want him to catch any illnesses."

So passed the autumn, winter, and spring, but during Jake's first summer, Martha stood her ground. "Other babies are not hidden away. And look how much he's grown. We've got to take him out sometime, don't we?"

Her papa, who had overheard the conversation, eagerly seconded Martha's idea.

"Sarah, let's do that. I need to pick up some lumber at the sawmill, and you and Mahthah can visit Adam Burke's dry goods store and walk around the village green a bit. What do you say?"

Reluctantly, her mama agreed. So on one hot Saturday, the family climbed into the buckboard behind their two brown horses, Molly and Max, and drove the short distance to town.

For Martha, Liberty Falls was just the right size. She loved the rectangular grassy village green, which marked the center of town and was alive with local farmers selling their produce and neighbors gossiping with each other. And she especially loved going with her mother to the dry goods store, the market, and the post office, which faced the green. Being somewhat shy and having to spend so much time watching Jake, though, Martha had not yet met a special friend of her own to play with on the green.

"I wish I had a friend to play with, Mama," she said.

Her mama looked surprised. "Thee has Jake, Martha."

Martha tensed her shoulders, but did not respond. There was no point.

On this first family outing, Martha felt it was most important for her to concentrate her attention on Jake and her mama. If they had a good time, maybe there would be lots more adventures away from the farm.

Her papa stopped their wagon in front of Adam

Burke's dry goods store and helped her and her mama down. Jake, in her mama's arms, craned his neck to look at all the new and interesting sights that Martha enjoyed pointing out to him.

As they entered the store, Martha gave a timid wave to Adam Burke, who took a moment to step from behind the counter to offer her a warm greeting. The shop owner was a gaunt, middle-aged Quaker man, who, for some reason Martha never could figure out, was called by both his names when anyone spoke about him. He always wore a serious expression on his face, which belied the keen sense of humor and generosity he often showed Martha and the other village children. Since he was president of the Liberty Falls Anti-Slavery Society, Martha worried that he might surmise the truth about Jake. But if he did, she was sure he would never reveal it to anyone.

"Good morning, Martha and Sarah. I've been waiting to welcome thy new family member. It's been such a long time since thee has been in. And, Sarah, we have not seen thee at Sunday meeting for months."

Her mama softly responded, "Thank thee, Adam, for thy thoughts. The child has been sickly, so we have kept to home."

Martha looked up at her mama's solemn expression and suddenly understood why she simply wanted to hide out at home and remain silent. In this way, she could avoid lying, which obviously pained her greatly.

"And thee, Martha," Adam Burke turned to her, leaning over so he could address her directly. "Are thee happy to have a little brother?"

"Yes," she squeaked out.

The kind man then reached for a huge jar he kept on the counter and offered Martha a small candy. She knew that being a free produce shopkeeper, Adam Burke would not sell any product made by the hands of a slave, including candy made from sugar. All of his delicious sweets contained honey or sugar made from local beets. So she was accustomed to seeing on the candy's wrapper the words:

Take this, my friend, you must not fear to eat.
No slave hath toiled to cultivate this sweet.

"Thank you," she muttered as her mama gently bumped her with her hip.

"And what can I get thee, Sarah?" he added as he returned to the counter.

"We need some diaper cloth, some soft homespun, perhaps in calico if thee has it, and wool to make baby dresses. Oh, and some end scraps for a baby quilt."

Martha noted that while Adam Burke helped her mama with her purchases, he took quick glances at Jake.

"He was thy cousin's son, Sarah?" he asked while wrapping her parcel.

Her mama kept her head down so low that the wide brim of her bonnet hid her bright red face. "Yes, from out near Torrington."

Adam Burke paused for just a moment, and Martha caught his meaningful glance. Then to her surprise he simply said, "I can see the family resemblance, especially to Martha." With that, he handed her the package. "That will be an even nine pence. The quilt scraps are my gift to the little lad."

After she paid for the purchases, Martha's mama again offered her thanks and hurried out of the store to where her papa waited with the buckboard. "That went very well, I think," she said.

Martha reached for her plait and twisted it around her finger.

"But, Mama," she asked, "isn't it strange that Mr. Burke thinks Jake looks like me?"

"Not at all," her mama answered. "It's thy black hair and tan skin. Do not dwell on it."

Martha wrinkled her brow in thought, but said no more. However, the next morning, feeling encouraged by the previous day's somewhat success, she asked, "Mama, are you going to meeting today? The Friends are wondering where you've been. And they haven't met Jake yet."

Once again, her papa agreed.

"Come, Sarah. I'll accompany you, and Mahthah can stay outside with Jake. Do you agree, Mahthah?"

Martha was starved for the outside world. Staying home all summer long was boring and made her resent taking care of Jake even more. "Oh, yes. Oh, yes, indeed."

And so once again the small family headed back to town. There Martha watched her parents go to the separate men's and women's sections of the Friends' meeting house to pray and meditate, while she sat down on the green lawn to try to keep Jake in one place. She definitely preferred the warm outdoors to sitting in silence inside the small white clapboard building with its hard wooden benches.

"Hello, Jakey," she smiled down on him as he clenched clumps of grass in his fists and tried to eat them. "No, no. Yech. Not in your mouth," she warned as she leaned over to pry the grass away. As soon as he started protesting, she stopped, but not before quickly wiping his hands.

"Hi, Martha," came a peppy voice behind her. It belonged to Becky Franklin, one of her schoolmates. "What've you got there? Is that your new brother? He's so small, just knee-high to a bumblebee."

"Yeah. He's about nine months old now."

"He's dear."

"Most of the time. But he's difficult to keep up with."

"I know about that," Becky shook her wild red hair out of her face. "Try watching five younger brothers and sisters just like him."

Martha laughed in surprise. She liked Becky. She was smart and, like herself, enjoyed school. But until now, the two of them had hardly spoken to each other. So having Becky approach her now was an unexpected pleasure.

"You the oldest?" Martha asked.

"Not quite. I suspicion that you've noticed my older brother Caleb in school. He's the real smart one. He's ten, works hard on the farm."

Becky looked sad for a moment.

"Something wrong?" asked Martha.

"Well, it's my papa. He doesn't really want Caleb to go to school. Says learning how to read and write is enough, and Caleb almost knows how to do that. Too much work on the farm."

"That's too bad."

Becky gave a small smile. "I help my mama with the house chores and taking care of the young 'uns,

but once I learn to read and write, I suspicion I'll
have to stop, too."

Martha looked at Becky with great compassion. Her
parents always told her how important learning was,
and they would never stop her from going to school.

"Is that why you pretend not to understand much at
school?" she asked.

Becky blushed. "Yeah. I hope no one else sees that."

"Well, I sure do. You might fool Miss Osgood, but
not me."

Becky laughed at that. Martha wished that she herself was as full of good humor as Becky always was.

"So, how come you're not in church, Becky?"

"I snuck out," she confided. "Got bored listening to the
reverend drone on and on about God and serving man-
kind and all that. I mean, I know it's important, but I
have so many other things I want to do. Like talk to you."

"I know what you mean," Martha replied happily.

"Oh! Do tell. I want to ask you something, Martha.
How come I see you going sometimes to my church
and sometimes to Quaker meetings?"

"And sometimes, none," Martha added. "My mama
is a Quaker. But she fell in love with my papa, who is
Unitarian."

Becky looked confused, so Martha explained further.
"Papa sometimes goes with Mama. That's where he is
today. And sometimes he goes to the Unitarians, but only,
he says, if there's a good anti-slavery sermon. Otherwise,
he says that faith is something you take care to live by
every day. He doesn't believe you have to go to church
to be a good person. And he doesn't believe Sundays are
special, either. So, sometimes I go and sometimes I don't."

"I like that, Martha. Wish I had folks like that."

"I do like Sunday school, though. I enjoy hearing the Bible stories and playing games with other children. But I don't seem to be going much these days because of Jake here."

"That's not so bad."

"I almost wish I could go to boring church instead of having to watch him all the time. He's always crawling around. And he is really, really fast, so I have to run and run and run all the time. He tires me out some."

"Speaking of which, Martha, where is he?"

"What do you mean? He's right behind me." But as she looked around, Martha saw exactly what Becky meant. Jake was gone. He was nowhere in sight.

"Oh, no!" she shrieked, and jumped to her feet in a panic. "I've got to find him. Becky, please, help me find him!"

Martha ran one way, then another, until Becky caught up and grabbed her arm.

"Martha, calm down. He's just been gone a minute, for pity's sake, and he can't have gone far. He's just a little thing. My brothers and sisters disappear at least once a day. And I always find them." Then Becky said with a mischievous look on her face, "Maybe the slave catchers got him."

Martha's face turned as white as a ghost. "Don't say that! Becky, why would you say that?"

"Martha, I was just jesting. Don't you know the game we play where one of us is the slave and the others the slave catchers? And the slave hides and the catchers have to find him?"

"No, I don't know it. And I don't want to play it. I've got to find him. Hurry!"

"My goodness," Becky sighed. "You sure are fretful."

Just as they headed for the back of the meeting house, Martha heard Jake's loudest wail of protest. She would know that sound anywhere. From around the corner of the building came a hefty, tallish boy with strawberry blond hair. He was carrying a struggling Jake across his shoulder like a sack of potatoes.

"Anyone missing something?" he asked.

"Me! Me! Please give him to me!" Martha cried out.

"Martha," Becky put in, "this is my brother, Caleb."

Caleb handed Jake over to Martha, turned on his heels, and stalked away.

"Thinks he's quite special," Becky said.

"Please thank him, Becky," Martha said with relief as she tried to comfort Jake. But he was too strong for her even at his size and his struggling knocked them both down, Martha landing with a resounding thud on her backside.

Becky laughed. "I've gotta skedaddle, Martha. See you in school."

"Thanks, Becky. And please remember to thank Caleb."

As soon as Becky left, Martha turned back to Jake, now flat on his back and flailing his arms and legs around. Before she could get him upright, her mama came running out of the meeting house. She scooped him up into her arms and hugged him tightly. Between his hiccups and gasps for breath, her mama wiped his tears and quietly asked Martha what had happened.

"Nothing, Mama. He was trying to eat some grass and then some pebbles, and I was taking them out of his mouth. So he had a fit." Another lie, but a good one, she thought, because it did not implicate her. This lying thing was getting easier and was pretty useful.

"Thee did the right thing, Martha. Micah, let us go home now, so I can quiet him down better."

FOR MARTHA, the weeks and months passed in a pattern just as reliable as the seasons usually were. Jake took his own sweet time, but Martha was relieved that by the age of two or so, he could walk and talk some. He was nowhere near as able as most children his age, but he was making progress. She tried as hard as she could to help him learn, but he was always too restless to stay in one place for long. He ran around the house, taking clothes out of drawers, utensils off the low wall by the hearth, and books and newspapers off tables and shelves. Martha was constantly cleaning up after him. He rarely went to sleep on time and often woke up in the middle of the night or very early in the morning or both, getting out of bed and making unintelligible loud noises. Since he shared a bed with Martha, she fell victim to his erratic behavior.

"Jake, get back to bed and go to sleep," she would insist. But it was all to no avail.

Jake also seemed to instinctively draw into himself and cower whenever a runaway slave was in the house.

Martha thought this unusual for such a curious and active child. She had no idea how he knew they were there or why this upset him so. To ease his anxiety, her papa took to hiding the fugitives in the haymow or in a carefully concealed spot he had created behind a stack of logs. Martha sometimes got to bring them food. Her heart went out to them, but she never had time to say more than a brief "Are you comfortable?" or "I hope you like this pie I helped my mama bake." Then she would hurry away, averting her gaze from their worried faces.

One sizzling summer night when Jake was almost three and Martha nine, her papa took them out to the dark field behind the house where they could easily see the sky full of stars. It was cooler there, and a soft breeze rustled the corn stalks nearby. Martha loved these outings with her father.

"Here, Jake, come lie between me and Mahthah and let's gaze up at the sky."

Jake clambered into their papa's arms, where he always seemed to feel safe and protected. "Stahs," he squeaked and pointed his little index finger straight up.

Her papa then took his son's finger gently, kissed it, and moved it toward the North, and Martha knew what would come next, for she had experienced this wonderful moment many times in her younger years. "See that big drinking gourd and long handle?" he asked Jake as he moved his finger to outline the cup. "See if you can follow those two stars on the gourd's edge. They point to that star right there. See it?"

Jake nodded, but Martha knew he probably could not make out any of the gourd's dipper-like shape. She certainly could not when she was his age.

"That," said her papa dreamily, "is the North Star. Slaves use it as a guide. And sometimes they sing spirituals about reaching the North and freedom." Gently, her papa let go of Jake's hand and, pushing himself onto his side, leaned on his bent arm and elbow. "Let's sing 'Swing Low, Sweet Chariot,' for Jakey, Mahthah, but real soft lest unfriendly ears be listening."

Martha nodded eagerly. And so they sang the song that Martha loved so much because it connected her so tightly to her papa:

> *Swing low, sweet chariot,*
> *Comin' for to carry me home.*
> *Swing low, sweet chariot,*
> *Comin' for to carry me home.*

And Jake joined in, ". . . low . . . home . . ."

After they finished the song, Martha wondered, as she often did, what had happened to Jake's mother after she left the South. Why was she all alone when she got to Uncle Jonah and Aunt Edith's house? Did she get left behind because she was having a baby? Or was she always alone? Maybe if someone had stayed with her, she would be alive and Jake would be in her arms and not in Martha's papa's, as things should be.

Once Jake had dropped off to sleep, Martha's papa stood up and lifted him tenderly in his arms.

"Time to head home, Mahthah. Your mama will be wondering what happened to us."

Martha got up and shook the grass off her skirt.

"Papa," she asked tentatively, "why is Mama always so sad and fretful?"

"It's nothing, my darling daughter. She is just concerned is all."

"About Jake?"

"Uh-huh."

"But why? He's safe with us, isn't he?"

"Of course, Mahthah. But she hears stories sometimes about slave catchers, and they frighten her. And also, she doesn't like to lie to people about where Jake came from."

"But people don't really ask questions anymore, do they?"

"Most don't," her papa said. "But there're still a few who stare at him and talk behind our backs. That's why she prefers staying home where she feels safe."

Martha thought about that for a while before speaking again. "Sometimes she seems angry at me, Papa. Doesn't she love me anymore?"

Martha's papa paused at the edge of the field and looked down at her with sorrow. "She loves you very much, Mahthah. She's just preoccupied. It's not just the slave catchers that worry her. It's also that it seems that Jake might not be growing up like normal children, and she doesn't know how to help him. She's worried that she's doing something wrong that's harming him somehow."

"Maybe that's why some people still notice him," Martha said.

"Maybe," her papa responded. "In any case, she keeps to herself. It's just easier for her that way."

Martha chewed the inside of her cheek as she thought this through. "Do you mean she frets because Jake doesn't seem to learn and is so jittery and can't sit still?"

"That and other things. You know how he is. He doesn't seem to understand the simplest instructions and he can't do the simplest things. Like holding a spoon the correct way. Or even making the easiest words into a sentence. And the way he moves his hands all the time, the same movement over and over again. And his swaying back and forth. Those sorts of things."

"Is that why she always makes me watch him? She thinks I can maybe teach him something?"

"No. I don't think she believes a girl can do better than a mama, even when that girl is good and responsible like you." He chucked Martha under the chin and gave her a big fatherly smile. "I just think that her feelings get low and Jake's running around and shrieking all the time tire her out."

"And she feels bad about it?"

"You're very smart, Mahthah. And exactly right. And she needs your help, so she asks for it."

Martha moved her teeth from her inner cheeks to her lips.

"I'll try to help more, Papa, but it's hard."

"I know. And I also know that somewhere down the road, Jake will grow out of this stage and be like any normal boy."

Martha sure hoped so. Meanwhile, the two walked slowly to the house, Martha looking down at the ground to hide her tears.

The one saving grace for Martha was that Becky had become her friend and a big help every Saturday and Sunday when the family went to town and they met up. There on the village green, they sat together, playing with their dolls or with Jake, pretending he was the baby. Jake, however, did not appreciate having to stay quiet and being swaddled like an infant. Once he mastered walking and then running, they had to change their games to suit him. Still, with Becky beside her, Martha had fun. The two friends chased Jake around or rolled a ball to him, which he could not catch even when he was four, then five. He was just all thumbs and constantly confused, turning this way and that, trying to figure out what he was supposed to be doing.

More often than not, Martha got tired of trotting after him or entertaining him, especially when she wanted to share secrets with Becky. So one Sunday when he was three, she got what she thought was a bright idea.

"Hey, Becky. I brought this piece of rope with me. I figure we can tie it around Jake's waist and then he can run around, but not run away."

"You are some pumpkins, Martha," she said as they fastened the long rope around Jake and then around the tree they were sitting under. Once they were sure he was secure, they got seriously involved in their game of cup and ball. Every so often, Martha glanced around to check on her brother or to accept some treasured leaf or rock he offered as a gift.

"Mattie," he would say, using his nickname for her. "Yook."

"Very nice, Jakey," she would answer and then hug him. "Now go play. Becky and I are busy."

Just as Martha tossed up the ball on its string and angled her cup under it for her winning point, she heard a familiar sound, one that reminded her of the day Jake was born—horses' hooves along with deep male voices laughing.

"Martha," Becky stammered, "I think those wicked slave catchers are back. They sometimes come through town like we live way out on the frontier. Why are they here, do you think?"

Martha started to gently pull Jake in by the rope. He had wandered way out to the full length of his tether, and the men had stopped and dismounted close to him.

"Well lookee here," Martha heard the bigger one say. "A little boy on a rope. Think he's a caught fugitive, Tom?"

"Might be, Will. Let's take a closer look."

As the two men moved toward Jake, Martha gave the rope a tug so hard that Jake fell and began to cry.

"Maybe you better run to the meeting house, Becky, and get my folks."

Becky nodded and took off at top speed. As she turned to look back, Martha saw her collide with Caleb, now at age twelve a reedy, gawky-looking farm boy.

"Whoa!" she heard him say. "What's the rush?"

"Slave catchers. Over there with Jake and Martha."

"What's the big deal? They have nothing to worry about."

"I'm not so certain. I gotta go get Martha's parents." And she ran away as fast as she could.

Martha glanced nervously at Caleb as she knelt by Jake and wiped the tears from his eyes, the snot from his nose, and then held him close. "Go away," she told the two men. "You're giving him a fright."

Will winked at his partner, leaned over Jake and

Martha, and bellowed, "This boy does look kinda brown to me."

"Well, he's the same color as me," Martha bellowed right back. "We're white. Go away!"

Caleb took this moment to stride over to the scene.

"Martha," he said in an agitated voice, "our folks told me to come and fetch you. It's past time to go home. Said you'd be in big trouble if you don't get a move on."

He reached for Jake and removed the rope. "Excuse me, gentlemen," he said, "my brother and sister have to leave now."

Martha was flabbergasted but she caught on right away to Caleb's ruse.

"Sorry, Caleb. I lost track of time."

Martha could tell that Caleb was having fun now with his role as rescuer. "Well, Mama and Papa are gonna tan your hide if we don't hurry. And they're gonna be vexed that you tied him up like a slave."

Martha opened her mouth in protest, then promptly shut it. Had she really done that?

Caleb lifted Jake, and he and Martha hastened across the village green, leaving the two men dumbfounded. They were so loud, however, that Martha clearly heard their ongoing conversation.

"You know, Tom, those two kids have a lotta gumption, but something about them doesn't smell right. Anyways, I'm tired of this town. Dawes keeps sending us back here, convinced he'll find that young filly, but I've never seen hide nor hair of anyone fitting her description."

"Me neither," added Tom. "And we won't neither

'cause these Connecticut Yankees know how to hide their runaways or pass 'em on north."

"You've got a point. I say we quit this town and head back home."

"For now, though, I'm mighty hungry," Tom said as the two men mounted their horses. "Let's go find some grub. We passed a place a few towns back. And maybe we can get us a good wash. I really need one."

"I'll say," responded Will as he slapped his horse on the rump with his reins.

As Martha and Caleb crossed the main road to the meeting house, the two men passed in front of them, waving their hats and grinning like hyenas as they headed south.

"A good direction for them," muttered Caleb.

"Thank you *so* much, Caleb. That's the second time you've come to Jake's rescue."

"It's nothing."

Martha was relieved that the slave catchers' affront had not fazed Jake in the least. Right then, he was busy getting a better look at Caleb. He patted Caleb's cheeks and hugged him around the neck, enjoying, as Martha herself did, the earthy smell of hay and cows that clung to his hair and clothes.

"Here. Let me take him," Martha offered.

"Nah," Caleb replied. "I'm used to young 'uns. My brothers and sisters climb all over me when we rough-house. But this skinny little fella sure feels light. He's just a little splinter. I like him." Much to Martha's surprise, Caleb gave Jake a big hug.

After that, on Sundays when Caleb came to town, he often stopped by during Becky and Martha's visits.

Martha was grateful that he sincerely liked to entertain Jake, and Jake responded with enthusiasm. As soon as he spotted Caleb, he ran to him, his arms reaching to be picked up for a hug and maybe even a ride on his shoulders. Martha wished she was young enough to do the same because even though she was only nine, she found Caleb interesting and exciting.

"Becky," Martha asked her friend soon after the episode on the village green. "What's it like to have an older brother?"

"It's fine, but he can be pretty bossy. Like you are with Jake."

"Oh."

"Martha," Becky ventured, "can I ask you something?"

"Sure. We're best friends, aren't we? You can ask me anything."

"Yeah." She paused. "I heard my parents say your folks hide runaway slaves. Is that true?"

Martha bit her lower lip and played with her hair as she considered her response carefully. What should she do? Tell the truth? After all, Becky was her best friend. Couldn't she trust her? Tell a lie like the ones that bothered her mama so? Neither? Slightly confused, she decided to do neither. Instead, she answered the question with one of her own.

"Sakes alive! Why did they say that?"

"Caleb told them about what happened the other week on the green."

"Oh."

"They wondered if your parents were attracting those wicked men to the town."

"My parents wouldn't do that."

"No. I didn't think so."

"Don't your parents hate slavery, Becky? Almost everyone around here does."

"Yeah, they do. But they don't get involved. You know what I mean? They say it's too dangerous. They just mind their own business."

"Just like my folks," Martha responded. "They just mind their own business, too."

Martha was happy to end the query. She had led Becky away from her main concern so easily that her friend seemed to lose track of her own question. And as for Martha, she felt relieved that she had not given away any secrets nor told any lies. But this keeping secrets business was getting really, really hard.

CHAPTER
5

IN SEPTEMBER 1850, Martha skipped to school every day as happy as could be. She was now ten years old and ready for new and harder subjects. While it was true that sooner or later she would have to go to a larger school with separate grade levels, for now she could enjoy the safety of her small, comfortable one-room schoolhouse.

Other parts of her life were going smoothly as well. For months, there had been no sign of the slave catchers. Jake, at four, was less frantic. He sat still during his meals before bolting off for here and there. He dressed himself, although many days he put his pants or shirt on backward and Martha had to turn them around. His conversation was basic, but at least he was talking and making sense. Best of all, her mama was less fretful and spent more time on Jake's care. All these things gave Martha new opportunities to be with Becky and to pursue their newest passion—knitting. Her mama had taught her to knit and purl over the summer, and at the moment, she was making a nice warm scarf for her papa.

One beautiful day as she skipped and sang on her way to school, Martha spotted the new issue of *The Liberator* on a chair in front of Adam Burke's store. Always curious, she stopped to look at some of the headlines. "The Law to Catch Men" immediately drew her attention. Something about it made her shiver involuntarily. Just then, Adam Burke came outside.

"I see thee finds my newspaper interesting, Martha," he said.

"I always enjoy looking at the story titles." She pointed to the article in question. "But, Mr. Burke, what does this one mean?"

"Ah. It's a bad day for us all. A new law just passed that gives slave owners and slave catchers the right to go anywhere in the nation and reclaim fugitives. It even says they can claim someone they *think* is a fugitive, and that person will need a lot of people to attest they are not."

Martha did not totally understand what Adam Burke meant, but she was late for school, so she bid him a good day and hurried off. Still, an unwanted worry entered her mind. Something about this new law felt like a threat to her, but she could not figure out what it was, except Jake's face kept appearing before her eyes.

As Martha entered the school, Miss Osgood gave her a severe look.

"You're late, Miss Martha Bartlett. What's your excuse?"

"Sorry, Miss Osgood. I just stopped to say hello to Adam Burke."

"Well, sit down. And, Martha, plan on visiting Mr. Burke *after*, not *before*, school."

"Yes, ma'am."

Martha was distracted the entire morning. What did Adam Burke mean? Didn't Connecticut have laws protecting runaway slaves? That's what her papa told her. And what did that mean when it came to Jake? Papa said Jake was free because he was born in Connecticut. So why was she so concerned all of a sudden? She puzzled over this even as Miss Osgood talked about the plans for next year's seventy-fifty anniversary celebration of the Declaration of Independence, something she was very, very interested in.

As Miss Osgood dismissed the children for luncheon, Martha looked up, confused. How had the morning passed so quickly? Slowly, she piled up her books and took out the cloth with her bread, cheese, and apple wrapped in it. As she stood and looked for Becky, who had to gather three of her younger siblings to look after, Miss Osgood's voice startled her.

"Martha, is something wrong?"

"No, ma'am," she mumbled.

"Your head's been in the clouds all morning. What is it?"

Martha looked at her teacher thoughtfully, weighing just what she could or could not say. Miss Osgood was about the same age as her mama and had the same gentle way about her, but Martha had never heard her say anything at all about slavery. Should Martha say anything then? Sometimes the whole situation simply perplexed her.

Just to be on the safe side, she said, "It's nothing, Miss Osgood. Truly."

"Well, all right, then. I'll see you after luncheon."

Martha caught up with Becky as she was cleaning up her food scraps while keeping an eye on her brothers and sister.

"What was all that about?" Becky asked.

Again, Martha hesitated. Becky also spoke little about slavery, except to say she was against it, but her parents felt it was none of their concern. Martha bit her lip and repeated what she had said to Miss Osgood.

"It's nothing, Becky. Truly."

The afternoon went no better than the morning. Even when reciting her multiplication tables, Martha's mind kept drifting back to what Adam Burke had said. "It's a bad day for us all." He had indicated that the slave catchers might be back, and more of them. And slave owners, too. And there would be nothing anyone could do about it. Martha could not help being frightened of those two slave catchers who had threatened Jake and of someone finding out about the secret surrounding him. Surely no one would come looking for one troublesome little boy, would they?

Martha walked home alone rather than running along with Becky and her rambunctious gang. As she passed Adam Burke's store, she saw a large notice tacked on the door:

EMERGENCY MEETING TONIGHT.
8 O'CLOCK.
REGARDING THE NEW FUGITIVE SLAVE LAW.
FRIENDS' MEETING HOUSE.

A large group of men and women had encircled Adam Burke and were discussing the news.

"This is a wicked, wicked law," said one.

Another responded, "And just months before the seventy-fifty anniversary of the Declaration of Independence. How could those who profess to love liberty and equality pass such an abomination?"

Martha picked up her pace, distancing herself from the crowd. This was scary indeed, and all she wanted was to get home as quickly as possible.

As she entered the parlor, however, she saw her mama and papa huddled on the sofa over a copy of the same *Liberator* as she had seen earlier. They were whispering earnestly to each other.

"Ah, Mahthah," her papa said, "we didn't hear you come in."

Martha dropped her books on the floor and ran to him, flinging her arms around his neck. "Papa, I'm scared."

"Why? What happened?"

"This new law. You know. About the fugitive slaves. People in town are all talking about it."

"Don't worry," he said. "There's nothing for you to be frightened of."

"But what does it mean . . ." she lowered her voice to a whisper, "about Jake?"

"Jake?" he responded. "This law has nothing to do with him."

Just as her papa completed this thought, Jake came downstairs, still sleepy from his nap. His presence put an end to their conversation.

Martha was the first to speak. "Come on, Jakey. Let's

go to the kitchen and have a cup of milk and a molasses cookie to help wake you up."

"Mattie," he asked as he sat by the table, "why's everyone so sad?"

"We're not sad, Jakey. Mama and Papa were just talking about farm business. I didn't really understand it all myself."

That evening after supper, Martha's papa went to town for the meeting. Her mama sat quietly in the parlor staring off into space, so Martha took Jake upstairs and tried to read him a story. After a page, he pushed the book closed.

"Jake, don't you want to know what happens to Joggy and Lorina after the nice woman in New York takes them into her home?"

"No," he said as he started jumping up and down on their feather mattress.

Martha put her hands on her hips and started tapping her foot. "Stop, Jake! You'll break the bed."

As always, he ignored her. He simply jumped and jumped, never tiring.

Martha's blood pumped with anger.

"Stop, Jake! Come on. It's time to go to sleep."

She reached out to grab him, but he easily evaded her grasp and laughed. Martha gritted her teeth and, her frustration at the boiling point, put her hands on her hips. "Do whatever you want. I'm sick and tired of you."

She stormed out of the room and scurried down to the parlor.

"Mama. Jake is jumping again. Can't you make him stop?"

Her mama paused in her staring. "He is doing no harm. Let him be."

"But he'll break the bed."

"No matter."

Martha was about to insist that her mama do something when her papa returned from town. Martha immediately took in the desolate look on his face.

"What is it, Papa?"

He sat down heavily next to her mama and, taking her hand, said in a soft voice, "Sarah, we need to speak." Her mama nodded but did not say a word. "And Mahthah, you're old enough to understand this as well."

Martha sat as her father shared his bad news.

"I didn't realize this before, but there's something dangerous for us in the new law," he said.

"What?" Martha asked.

"It says that anyone who hides a fugitive or tries to prevent one from being captured can be fined up to one thousand dollars and serve up to six months in prison. You can see that it'll now be impossible for us to help runaway slaves on their route north. Doing so will put us in jeopardy and could draw attention to Jake."

"Why?" asked Martha. "Isn't he free?"

"Yes," her papa said. "But his mother's master would not see it that way. And if the wrong people put two and two together, they could report their claim that Jake was born of a slave woman and quite possibly receive a reward."

Martha saw her mama close her eyes, a big tear escaping from one. "My boy," she said sadly.

"And there'll be slave catchers and kidnappers aplenty up North. We'll have to keep an extra careful watch on Jake. Mahthah," he added as he glanced at her mama gazing into the fire, "this responsibility will fall heavily upon you."

Just as Martha nodded her assent, she heard a loud crash from upstairs. "I think Jake has just broken the bed."

"I'll tend to it," her papa said. He unwrapped his hand from her mama's, kissed her on the forehead, and walked slowly upstairs.

For a while, Martha sat by her mama's side thinking about what her papa had said. She felt frightened, worried, tired, and vexed all at the same time. Would those slave catchers be back? Would a neighbor looking for some much needed money decide to sell information about Underground Railroad workers or runaways? Or about Jake? He might irk her beyond endurance, but, still, he was her brother and she loved him to distraction. She would be extra vigilant now so that no harm could come to him.

Surely, her papa must be exaggerating his fears, especially about the kidnappings. But to be certain, Martha decided to find out for herself. As copies of *The Liberator*, *The North Star*, and *Charter Oak* arrived, she carefully examined them for articles about kidnappers. She then clipped each one out and placed it in the wood keepsake box her papa had made for her.

In January of that winter, 1851, Martha saw her first evidence of a child having been kidnapped. She moved her face close to the print, her lips moving as she read. "Oh, no! Poor boy," she muttered in a voice she thought only she could hear. "'G. F. Alberti and

others seized, under the Fugitive Slave Law, a free colored boy, named Joel Thompson, alleging that he was a
slave. The boy was saved.' Thank goodness for that!"

"Who are you talking to, Mattie?" Jake asked as he
played with his toys.

"No one, Jake. Just myself."

A week later, Martha again muttered aloud,
"Clearfield County, Pennsylvania, about January
twentieth. A boy was kidnapped and taken into slavery." So her papa's fears were correct. Martha was
nearly paralyzed with fright. Except when she was in
school, she never let Jake out of her sight. By the end
of the first week, she was exhausted, but she never
gave up her watch, not even when he wandered the
freezing house in the middle of the night, and, shiv-
ering, she followed after him.

As winter set in, Martha took to hiding inside her
home. It grew so cold that often she even succeeded
in convincing Jake to come to bed early so they
could snuggle together under her several quilts. The
only painful part was when Jake had to urinate into
the chamber pot. He would rush back into bed as
quickly as he could, immediately resting his cold feet
on the small of Martha's back to warm up.

"Thanks," she'd mutter irritably.

As snow and ice accumulated, Martha's isolation
grew more pronounced. She spent much time chip-
ping ice off the water pump and in the spring room
barrel, feeding the chickens, milking the cows, and
bringing firewood in for the stove and fireplace, all
the while insisting Jake stay by her side.

As her mama grew more anxious, she withdrew

into a world of silence and disconnectedness. Martha, therefore, took on more cooking and household responsibilities as a means of helping her and quite simply to be near her. She thought that her chatty presence might cheer her mama up, but more often than not, it did not. In her very few spare moments, she searched the newspapers for kidnapping notices rather than paying attention to her schoolwork. The results were disastrous as she gave Miss Osgood wrong answers when asked questions and failed several tests.

Only Martha's papa acted his usual self as he made regular trips to the shops in town and the sawmill. When the roads were halfway passable, after breakfast he took her to school in his wagon or on horseback and in the afternoon picked her up. When she was at school, she spent her time fretting over Jake. Would her mama keep her eye on him? Would she be able to protect him if a stranger came looking for him when her papa was away on errands?

There was one bright spot for Martha that winter. Just one. Sometime in February, her papa walked in carrying a stray cat. She was a dear little thing, with soft black fur and a white oval on her face. "Here, children," he said. "I found this little runaway and thought we might take her in."

Martha was thrilled and grabbed for the cat, snuggling her to her chest. She could feel the vibration of her purr and her quick heartbeat. As Jake jumped up and down trying to reach the kitty, she pushed him away.

"Mahthah," her papa said. "Share."

Not happy, but always obedient, Martha sat Jake down and placed the animal in his lap. "Catty," he said. "Let's call him Catty."

Martha grumbled. Her papa gave her a look.

"She's a female cat, Jake. How about Miss Catty?"

And so they agreed, and although Miss Catty was supposed to be their joint responsibility, Martha fed her and cleaned up after her. Together, she and Jake petted and played with her for hours. Before long, she was one of the family.

One evening at supper time, Miss Catty jumped right onto the table and then onto Martha's papa's shoulder. "Why, this is a cat-astrophe!" he punned. Martha started to giggle.

"Why, that animal cat-apulted right onto my shoulder!" he added in mock shock. Martha laughed and Jake chimed in. Even Martha's mama laughed.

"Why, if she doesn't get off me, I may succumb and have to be buried in the cat-acombs!" he continued. He then gently lifted the creature off his shoulder and placed her on the floor.

By this time, of course, the house was filled with mirth, wrapping Martha in a cocoon of love and warmth. Throughout the cold winter, Miss Catty entertained Martha and took her mind off her troubles. She sometimes even enjoyed sharing her with Jake. But soon spring came with its beautiful flowers and trees and muddy roads and black flies.

To Martha's great dismay, Miss Catty disappeared into the barn and fields, returning home only occasionally for a bowl of fresh milk. Now an outdoor cat, she avoided Martha's attempts to hold her, leaving her feeling bereft.

To add to her unhappiness, one day at school, Becky cornered Martha.

"Martha, I never see you on the green anymore."

"It was winter, Becky. Too cold to be out."

"But winter is over now, and I've been looking for you every Saturday and Sunday. And you missed so much school this winter. Were you sick?"

"No, not exactly. I was just cold. And the snow was so deep."

"I dunno. I got here. Anyway, wanna meet on the village green on Sunday?"

"I'm not sure, Becky. My mama's been ill. She hasn't gone to meeting lately, so I'll most likely stay home."

"I see," muttered Becky. "Guess I'll see ya sometime, then."

Martha could feel her friend's hurt as Becky walked away. She too felt bad, but taking care of Jake by herself on the village green scared her. Until her mama worked up her courage to go back to meeting, Martha preferred to watch over Jake at home even if it meant missing spending time with Becky or working on the Independence Day anniversary plans.

And in any case, the springtime of 1851 was busier than usual, and Martha had much to do. There were more requests for Martha's papa's woodworking skills, so it fell to her to feed all the animals and bring in all the firewood. She also needed to keep Jake out of sight as more strangers came to the woodshop. People needed new farm utensils and repairs to furniture damaged during the winter. New babies called for cradles and little chairs. Her papa created beautiful and useful items for these families to enjoy, and his reputation spread far beyond the borders of Liberty Falls.

One day he announced, "I've decided to take on a part-time helper in the woodshop."

"Who?" her mama, concerned about strangers, asked.

"Caleb Franklin. He's nearly fourteen now and his father's anxious for him to learn a skill that might be useful on the farm. The family's large and can also use some extra money."

Martha's heart skipped a beat at the thought of Caleb being so close. "Would he be here every day?" she asked.

"Six days in the winter," her papa replied. "Almost full days in the summer, and as time permits during planting and reaping seasons. Of course, not on Sunday. It's not perfect, but he'll be a great help."

"Well, Jake," Martha said, "looks like Caleb will be here a good amount of time."

Jake grinned and clapped his hands.

A few weeks later, Martha saw Caleb saunter onto the farm to begin his learning. Before she could stop him, Jake dashed out the front door and threw himself around his legs.

"Whoa, little splinter," Caleb laughed. "I'm not here to play. It's work time for me."

"Jacob," her mama called. "Thee leave Caleb alone now."

Martha rushed out to retrieve Jake, but he would not let go. Instead, he just clung on tighter. Seeing a fit on its way, Martha made a proposal. "Let's do this. When it's time for luncheon, we can carry Papa and Caleb's food to them, as Papa doesn't like to stop work for too long a time."

"And," added her papa, who had come to welcome Caleb, "the three of you can take an hour to enjoy the nice weather."

Until noon arrived, Martha kept an eye on Jake, who ran endlessly around the house and the yard. When she eventually gave him the cheese, bread, apples, and water to carry to the woodshop, he teetered under the weight of it. She carefully took the water and apples from him and they headed off. From that day on, up to an hour each midday, Martha, Caleb, and Jake shared food. Then they either played tag or bat-the-ball in the farmyard or wandered off to a nearby stream that fed into Blackwell's Brook to dip their feet into the cool, refreshing water.

One hot day after enjoying the stream, Martha saw Adam Burke's buckboard pull up to the woodshop. Her mama greeted him and then took a protesting but tired Jake inside for a nap. Martha and Caleb, however, hung back, sitting for a short while on a bench under an open window of the shop. As they were about to talk to each other, they heard Adam Burke greet Martha's papa.

"Micah, may I speak with thee about something sensitive?"

"Of course, Friend. What is it?"

"The Friends are concerned because we haven't seen Sarah or thee at meetings for quite some time. And Martha hasn't been on the village green to meet her friend, Becky, or at Sunday school, for that matter. In fact, we see little of thee at all. Is there some trouble here at home we can help thee with?"

"No, but thank you for your concern, Adam. We're fine."

There was an uncomfortable silence during which Martha tried to lure Caleb out of earshot.

"Caleb, I'm thirsty. Would you walk me over to the well?"

"Oh, no, Martha. Don't try to move me. This sounds really, truly interesting."

"I think it might be wrong for us to listen in on my papa and Adam Burke. Let's go elsewhere."

"No." Caleb was quite stubborn and persistent.

Martha heard Adam Burke clear his throat. "Micah. Many of us know what the situation here is. We want thee to know that we're all watching out for thee. That we'll keep our eyes open so that Martha and Jake, especially, are never out of someone's sight or hearing."

"I don't know what you're referring to," her papa stammered.

"Yes. I believe thee does. Just know," he added, "it's not healthy for thee to sequester thyselves. The children must have as normal a life as possible."

Another silence followed. Martha caught Caleb staring at her, his eyebrows lifted into an arc. "What's he talking about?" he whispered.

"I'm not sure. Maybe it's that I've been so scared by those slave catchers that I'm afraid to walk to school alone."

"But they haven't been around here for almost a year. I suspicion they found plenty of fugitives to chase elsewhere since the law was passed."

"Perhaps, but I prefer to stay here on the farm where I feel safe. And now that you're here, I have no need to go further."

Martha blushed as Caleb smiled.

"But soon you'll have to return to school."

"Perhaps Papa'll take me there and pick me up."

"Or maybe I can walk you one or both ways when I can get away."

Martha felt elated to have Caleb's attention and relieved because he had not learned the truth behind her family's fears. And yet, she was also regretful because once again she had been untruthful. It would make her life so much simpler if she could just share Jake's story with Caleb. And Becky, too.

Finally she again heard her papa speak. "Thank you, Adam. I'll tell Sarah what you've said and reassure Martha that it's safe for her to visit with Becky Franklin on the village green. You're a true friend to us."

"Many in town are true friends to thee," responded Adam Burke as he headed to his buckboard.

Although Martha's mama reluctantly agreed to return to Sunday meeting, Martha preferred to watch Jake at home. If he could, Caleb joined her. If her mama or papa went to town on Saturdays, she went along but would not linger on the village green, even with Becky, unless Caleb was there. And so passed the rest of 1851, 1852, and much of 1853, years during which Martha and Caleb's friendship grew. By 1853, when Martha turned thirteen and Caleb sixteen, fondness and an understanding led each to believe that sometime in the future they might become more than just friends.

But those years were not easy ones for Martha. Jake started school in the fall of 1851, and Martha had her hands full. He was not the kind of child who sat quietly and listened to the teacher. Instead, he was the same as he had always been at home. Very active. Very naughty. He could not sit still for more than ten minutes at a time. He had little patience for learning and remained unable to grasp even the simplest skills. Recitation so confused him that Martha wondered if he would ever learn his letters or numbers, much less how to read.

"Jake, don't you like reading?" she asked him one day.

"No," he responded.

"Why not?"

"The letters squiggle around and they don't make any sense."

Martha approached her parents about Jake's school problems. "He has a tremendous will of his own," she told them. "He's very passionate in school and Miss Osgood can't control him. I've heard some children call him names and imitate his swaying and hand motions. They're mean to him and that makes me very angry."

"Don't worry so much, Mahthah. I'm sure things will improve now that he's in school," her papa assured her. "Soon these fits of disobedience will subside and he'll take off and start to understand. After all, he's had a difficult start to his life, and maybe all of our watching him so closely has some-how prevented him from maturing."

"I don't agree," she complained. "He's had the same upbringing as me. And when he misbehaves, I'm the one who's called upon to quiet him and get him to sit still. Then I can't concentrate on my own studies, which I love so much."

"Please, Martha," her mama said. "Be patient with

our boy. I'll talk with him and help him with his lessons at home so thee can do thy studying."

Martha was unsure of her mama's offer. She knew her attempt to help Jake would not last for long. And she was right. Jake continued to misbehave at home, in school, and on the village green, and her mama continued to grow more unsteady until she was of no real practical help to Martha. Her papa could control Jake, but he was too busy to stop work to discipline him on a regular basis. Only when Caleb sat him down and talked with him or told him a story would Jake retain a little bit of self-control.

"Jake," Caleb said one day when he came to walk him and Martha home from school. "Were you a good boy today?"

"No," Jake laughed. "I dropped my slate and it broke, so Miss Osgood made me stand in the corner. I did that, but when she wasn't looking at me, I turned around and made faces so the other children would laugh."

Martha frowned.

"Jake," responded Caleb. "Be a good boy in school. If you aren't, I won't be able to play with you after my work is done."

"Why not?"

"Because your mama and papa will be angry at you and won't allow you to play."

"They won't be angry. They are *never* angry. Only Mattie gets angry."

"But Jake, you don't want *me* to be angry with you, do you?" asked Caleb.

"No. Never. I love you, Caleb."

"Then be good."

Martha felt truly grateful for Caleb's attempts to help her with Jake. And to his credit, Jake tried, but he was never able to be as good as most children in the school. Caleb would not speak to him on days when Martha told him Jake had misbehaved. Like the time Jake put a frog under Miss Osgood's book, which jumped at her when she picked it up. Or when he tied Jane Appleton's shoestrings together so that when she got up to walk, she fell flat on her face. The class roared with laughter while poor Jane could only rub her sore nose for the rest of the day. Martha truly believed that Jake would never be able to be schooled and that was what made him misbehave. She felt sorry for him, but sometimes, she felt sorrier for herself.

Miss Osgood tried to help by visiting Martha's mama and papa, but her papa stuck to his usual response. "I'm sure Jake will grow out of it. I'm positive he won't be playing such pranks when he's a grown man. In the meantime, we'll do our best to help him with his lessons."

Martha simply believed her parents preferred to lie, this time to themselves. In the meantime, her own concern over Jake forced her to continue to search for clippings about kidnappings. She was unable to stop herself even though the notices upset her. In October 1852, John Henry Wilson was taken from Pennsylvania, and not found, and in July 1853, a girl of just four or five was kidnapped from Providence, Rhode Island. Martha felt certain that the kidnappers were coming closer.

Then that fall, a notice was posted on buildings and fence posts all over Liberty Falls.

$200 REWARD
FOR INFORMATION
ABOUT A RUNAWAY SLAVE.

YOUNG, BEAUTIFUL WOMAN
IN HER EARLY TWENTIES.
ANSWERS TO THE NAME MARIAH.
VERY LIGHT SKIN AND
LONG WAVY BLACK HAIR.
OF THIN STATURE.
ABOUT FIVE FEET SEVEN INCHES.
ALMOND-SHAPED HAZEL EYES.
WITH CHILD WHEN LAST SEEN.
CHILD WOULD NOW BE
SEVEN YEARS OLD.

$200 FOR ANY INFORMATION
LEADING TO HER RECOVERY
AND $100 MORE FOR THE CHILD.

CONTACT ROBERT DAWES AT
LAGRANGE PLANTATION,
DORCHESTER COUNTY, MARYLAND.
DATED: NOVEMBER 24, 1853.

Martha and her parents were stunned. Never before had anyone tried to find Jake and his mother in such an aggressive manner. The slave catchers that had come through town about once a year were no doubt the hirelings of this man, Robert Dawes. After all, Martha had once heard them use Dawes's name. But they had been all bluster and not at all effective in their quest. So, why

$200 REWARD

FOR INFORMATION ABOUT A RUNAWAY SLAVE

YOUNG, BEAUTIFUL WOMAN IN HER EARLY TWENTIES. ANSWERS TO THE NAME

MARIAH

VERY LIGHT SKIN AND LONG WAVY BLACK HAIR. OF THIN STATURE. ABOUT FIVE FEET SEVEN INCHES. ALMOND-SHAPED HAZEL EYES. WITH CHILD WHEN LAST SEEN. CHILD WOULD NOW BE SEVEN YEARS OLD.

$200 FOR ANY INFORMATION LEADING TO HER RECOVERY AND $100 MORE FOR THE CHILD.

CONTACT ROBERT DAWES
AT LAGRANGE PLANTATION,
DORCHESTER COUNTY, MARYLAND

DATED: NOVEMBER 24, 1853

now? Had someone or something led him to believe that his runaway slave was still alive and in the United States, not dead or safely in Canada? Whatever his reasons, this notice gave Martha terrifying nightmares.

One evening, her papa took her aside.

"Dear Mahthah," he said, "you must not allow this notice to take over your life. Just as in the past, the slave catchers or this Robert Dawes himself will find nothing and disappear."

"But, Papa," Martha sobbed, "the description is exactly Jake. The almond-shaped hazel eyes. The fair skin. The age. And now we have a name for his mama . . . Mariah. Such a pretty name."

"That description could fit a number of runaways. It'll lead to nothing."

"And Jake," Martha added, "does many bad things to draw attention to himself."

"If he was quiet and sullen," her papa noted, "he might make himself even more conspicuous."

While Martha mulled this over, her papa pressed on.

"Mahthah, you must act as if nothing has changed. Calm down. And do nothing different."

"But I'm frightened, Papa. I want only to stay home and not venture out."

"No. I'll see you and Jake safely to school and then back home. Or I'll send Caleb. Just as we do now. Understand?"

"Yes, Papa."

"In the meantime, try to do something you enjoy and *do not* read any more of my newspapers."

Martha was surprised that he had noticed her clandestine activity. "Yes, Papa."

But Martha still had one copy of *The National Anti-Slavery Standard* reporting the kidnapping of a fourteen-year-old white girl, a girl just like her. Only in the nick of time was the error found, the girl released, and the abductors arrested. And then another snatching, this time of Jack, a nine-year-old black boy taken from Boston to Selma, Alabama, into slavery. She could not help but notice the similarity. Jack. Jake. One letter. Just one little letter.

NOVEMBER WAS fraught with worry, but December held promise because it was the month of the Liberty Falls annual Anti-Slavery Fair. Martha loved everything about this annual fund-raising tradition, especially since girls and boys her age indulged themselves in a bit of flirting and even court-ing. A few days before the grand event, Martha care-fully passed a note to Becky during school. "Can't wait to see you at the fair this weekend. Your folks will let you go, won't they?"

Becky wrote back. "Yeah, because it's in our church. Maybe I'll meet a nice boy there."

Martha could not help giggling. She and Becky were both thirteen now and courting was just beginning for them. She answered, "Will Caleb be there?"

"Oh, yes. He's my official chaperone."

"Martha. Becky," came the stern voice of Miss Osgood, who suddenly towered over them, "may I have the note please."

Martha handed it over as Miss Osgood added, "One

more time and you'll be staying after school to clean the slates and sweep the floors."

"Yes, ma'am," Martha replied, giving Becky a secret smile before returning to her math problems. How could she *not* smile with the fair just a few days away?

The evening of the event, Martha put on the new green and red plaid wool dress that her aunt Edith had made for her. Her mama added a pretty white crocheted lace collar, which Martha thought made the dress even fancier. Just as she started brushing out her long, straight black hair, her mama, a big smile splashed across her face, came to her door.

"Thee looks lovely, Martha," she said. "Shall I help to fix thy hair?"

Martha was thrilled to see her mama looking so happy. "Oh, yes, Mama. I love it when you brush my hair."

"It looks so nice hanging loose down thy back. Shall we leave it unplaited and just tie it with this?" She then produced a width of green and red striped ribbon, the most luxuriant Martha had ever seen.

Martha beamed as she ran her fingers along the satiny fabric. "Thank you so much, Mama. It's beautiful."

"Thee is a great help to me, Martha, and I love thee more than I can say. Tonight, do not worry. Thy papa and I shall tend to Jake."

As Martha enjoyed the feel of the brush in her mama's hands, she said, "Becky always teases me about my plaits. She says they are so long that they make me look like an Indian."

Martha felt her mama pause, then begin brushing again. "Well, Becky Franklin does not know everything. Thy hair is like that of many other girls."

"But I always wondered, Mama, how come you have your blonde hair and Papa his bright blue eyes, and I have black hair and brown eyes?"

"I'm sure that somewhere back in time, someone in our family had these same traits," her mama replied as she tied the ribbon. "Thee is ready. Let us find Jake and thy papa and be on our way."

Within minutes, they were all gathered near the door. Martha wrapped her warm woolen shawl around her shoulders and then grabbed two heavy quilts for her and Jake to snuggle under during the cold ride into town. As the buckboard slipped and slid its way over the icy roads, she and Jake sang the simple songs she had taught him, especially his current favorite, "Long, Long Ago."

Within minutes, it seemed, they were in the warm, cheerful church basement with friends and neighbors talking and laughing together among the colorful booths displaying handmade goods for sale. The sweet smell of apple cider and fresh-baked maple doughnuts made Martha's mouth water, and she longed to eat one of the sweet cakes. Maybe two. Perhaps three.

The first person she spied was her aunt Edith, who promptly took her aside.

"Here, my beautiful niece, is a little gift to help you enjoy the fair."

Martha accepted the small handmade crocheted purse that matched the collar of her dress. Inside were several coins.

"Oh, Aunt Edith. Thank you so much."

"Your mama looks so cheerful tonight, Martha. I'm glad. Now, you go and have fun. I'll help with Jake."

Martha opened her mouth to speak, but Aunt Edith cut her off. "Go. I see your friends looking for you."

Martha gave Aunt Edith a hug and turned to see Becky and Caleb wending their way through the crowd toward her. They were grinning from ear to ear.

"Martha," Caleb and Becky said in one voice, "come on. There's lots to do."

"Can I, Mama?" she asked.

"Of course, child. Thee have a pleasant time."

Released of all responsibility, Martha happily hurried off, pulling Becky by the hand.

"First stop. Maple doughnuts. Second. Cider."

"Absolutely," Becky responded.

Once Martha, Becky, and Caleb had each chomped down three sweet treats, Martha looked around at the booths. What could she buy with her shiny new coins?

"I want to purchase some gifts," she said excitedly. "First, for my papa."

Caleb pointed to a booth selling pen wipers for blotting excess ink off a piece of paper. Each had an inscription. "How about one of these? You can choose between 'Wipe Out the Blot of Slavery,' or 'Plead the Cause with Thy Pen.'"

"I think the blot message is stronger."

After Martha handed over her three pence for the wiper, she grabbed Becky's hand to show her a handmade wooden needle holder.

"Look at these, Becky. Do you think my mama would like one?"

"I sure do," Becky said. "I know mine would. If I had the money, I'd buy one myself."

Martha took a few of the remaining coins from her purse and offered them to her best friend.

"No, Martha. Thanks, but you buy it. I'm knitting my mama a warm shawl anyway."

Martha then bought the needle holder, which came with a message written on a small sheet of paper: "May the use of our needles stick the consciences of slave holders."

"Now for Jake," she said. "I know exactly what I want. When I was little, Mama and Papa gave me *The Anti-Slavery Alphabet*. I loved the book, but one day I dropped it in the mud and that was that."

"I remember that book," said Caleb. "I used to read it each year during the fair. It was pretty serious. Do you think Jake would like it?"

"The sentences are short and the drawings of the letters eye-catching, so maybe he would. I'm trying anything I can think of to help him to read."

Sure enough, the small book was prominently displayed on the literature table.

After paying for it, Martha turned back to join her friends. But Becky was not there.

"She went bouncing off with Mark Griffen," grinned Caleb. "Said she'd see us later."

Martha blushed as Caleb took her hand. "Let's go somewhere private to talk." Her heart pounded as he led her to a side room next to where the coats were stored. It was dimly lit, quiet, and cozy feeling, and most noticeably, no one was anywhere near it. Martha was unsure about being with Caleb away from her mama and papa's eyes. They might disapprove and reprimand her for it, but she could not resist her urge to be alone with him.

"Martha," he began in a shy voice while he toyed with her fingers, "I know we're young. But I'm almost seventeen now and I think I can see what my future will be like. I'm hoping in a year or two we might court and think about being together."

Martha choked out, "Me too, Caleb."

"I bought you a little present to mark the start of our private pledge." And with that he gave her a small package. Martha looked down so Caleb would not see her red face as she carefully unwrapped the paper, revealing a beautiful handmade white silk handkerchief embroidered with a red rose. Immediately, she unfolded the soft fabric and rubbed it against her cheek.

Caleb smiled, moved closer, took Martha's face into his hands, and kissed her very lightly on the forehead, then the lips. She relaxed as her body tingled with pleasurable feelings she had never experienced before. Her first kiss. It was really, really nice, but embarrassing for some reason. Flustered, she took a very small step backward and said, "We'd better return to the fair before my papa comes looking for us."

Caleb nodded, took her hand, and together they left the peaceful room for the clamor and brightly lit lanterns of the main hall. Martha had never felt so happy and calm in her life. She gently squeezed Caleb's fingers before releasing them and moving a short distance away from him, as was proper.

Immediately, however, Martha could tell that something was amiss. Her papa and mama were having an animated conversation with Adam Burke, and as soon as her papa saw her, he rushed to her side. Taking no notice of her flushed face, he quickly said, "Excuse me, Caleb, but I need to have a word with Mahthah."

"Yes, sir. Is anything wrong?"

"It's nothing for you to fret over. Please, excuse us."

Taking Martha aside, he whispered close to her ear, "The slave catchers and a strange man in a rich-looking carriage have been seen in town asking questions. It's said to be Robert Dawes. Jonah, Edith, and Ned are leaving now and taking Jake home with them 'til it's safe for him to return. Your mama and I will see them off and then I'll come back for you. Please be ready to leave."

Giving her a reassuring pat on the back, her papa hurried off with her mama and Jake. Martha stood watching, her body trembling with fear. Caleb came up next to her and felt her shaking.

"What is it, Martha?" He paused, but she kept her silence. "Tell me. You can trust me with anything."

Martha led him back to the private room where they had so recently expressed their growing attachment to each other. She knew she should not reveal her family's secret. Yet she could no longer hold it in. Checking that no one else was nearby, Martha carefully closed the door and, in the quietest voice she could muster, told him Jake's story. To her great distress, Caleb showed no sign of surprise.

"Becky always thought there was something unusual in Jake's looks," he said, "and how you all have been so protective of him, especially when those slave catchers affronted you. It makes sense now."

Instantly, Martha grew anxious. How many other people in town guessed Jake's story? Had she somehow betrayed him? Had she just betrayed him again?

"Please, Caleb. Don't say anything, not even to Becky."

"I won't, Martha. I promise." He took her hand and squeezed it gently.

Reluctantly, Martha pulled her hand away, went next door to the coat room to retrieve her shawl, and left to meet her parents, who were waving farewell to Jake. As she looked back, she saw Caleb standing by the church door, his head hung low in deep concentration.

When the family's buckboard reached the snow-covered road to their farm, Martha spotted a black phaeton sitting outside their house. Its large, thin iron wheels and leather seats and carriage top reflected the apparent wealth of its owner. Flanking it were two men standing beside their horses. Martha recognized them immediately from their stances and the sneers on their travel-worn faces. They were Will and Tom, the slave catchers. She took in a deep breath as her papa maneuvered the buckboard to rest in front of the phaeton.

Robert Dawes unfolded himself from the cramped seat and stood next to the carriage. Martha stared at him with fascination. She had never seen a Southern gentleman before, and this one, although tired looking, was obviously well tended. He was about the same age and height as her father, she guessed, with fine features—a chiseled nose and sharp chin and a shock of black curly hair that dipped onto his forehead. He wore a brown wool chesterfield with a velvet collar, and on his head sat a stovepipe hat. His hands and feet were covered in soft brown leather. He was just like a picture from one of Martha's books about the evils of slavery.

Handsome, sleek, and untrustworthy. Martha strained to make out the words he spoke in a soft, musical-sounding accent. "Are you Micah Bartlett?"

"I am. And you are?"

"I thought you might have guessed that by now," he responded.

During the brief pause that followed, Dawes gave his horse an affectionate pat. Martha imagined he reserved such soft gestures for animals, not humans.

Her papa responded in a tough, serious voice Martha had never heard him use before. "From your accent, I would say you're a traveling peddler of some sort, and I have no interest in what you're offering."

"Of course you jest, Mr. Bartlett. I'm the owner of one fugitive slave by the name of Mariah and her young child. Do you remember them?"

"I've never known any fugitive with that name and don't know of her child. Is it a boy or a girl?"

Dawes ran his gloved hand around the back of his neck and gazed out over the dark, snow-covered fields. To Martha's surprise, he looked as sad and thoughtful as her mama when she stared into nothingness.

"In all likelihood, a boy. At least, that's what I've been told. The girl was with child when she ran away. In the last stages, I would say. Anyway," he snapped out of his reverie, giving Martha a start, "I've come to claim my property. And I believe they're here. I've brought my men to help look for them."

"This is private property, Mr. Dawes. You're not free to search it. In any case, the individuals you describe are not here."

Martha and her mama grabbed hands as Dawes

twisted his mouth and looked directly at them. "Under the Fugitive Slave Law, my men here have the right to search your property."

Martha cringed as the two rough-looking men took a threatening step closer to her papa. His back stiffened, and he took a deep breath before speaking. "I'll show you around. I expect you not to disturb anything."

The dark cold of the night seeped into Martha's bones, but she did not, could not, move, as her papa took one of the wagon's lanterns and led Dawes and his men to the barn and through the woodshop. What would she do if they harmed him?

As her gaze followed the movement of the lantern, her mama shook her arm. "Martha," she whispered. "Hurry into the house and hide Jake's toys and cover his clothing with some of thine own."

Martha did not leave the wagon or move her eyes from where her papa had just disappeared with Dawes and his men in tow.

"Come on. Move," her mama hissed.

Reluctantly, Martha climbed to the ground, but before entering the house and rushing upstairs, she asked, "Who would've told Dawes about Jake, Mama?"

"I do not know," she responded. "Perhaps someone desperately needs that reward money."

Martha quickly entered her room, hid Jake's things, and returned downstairs in time to see the men reach the house. They pushed their way past her and looked in each room, rustling pillows, pulling open cupboards, and, spying the attic, climbing the stairs and stomping around. Martha and her parents dogged them each step of the way.

"Who do you keep in the attic?" Dawes asked.

"It's empty as you can see," her papa answered. "Sometimes a guest will stay there."

"A guest," Dawes said, "of what complexion?"

No one answered him.

It seemed like hours before the search was over and the three men left the house. In the dark void of the yard, Martha heard Robert Dawes's final demand. "I have information that there's a young boy here that fits a similar description to the woman I'm seeking. Where is he?"

"There's no boy here now. My son's currently visiting relatives, but he is *my* son and not the child you seek."

"I'll be back to take a look at him."

After they departed, Martha's papa closed the door and secured it with a wooden bar. Never in her life had she known him to do so. Their door was always open to friends and strangers alike.

"Will they be back?" Martha asked.

"I don't know," her papa replied.

"Did they do any damage?"

"They just threw some hay around and threatened to destroy some furniture, but it was mostly bluster."

Martha collapsed on the sofa where her mama tried to comfort her. "Do not worry, Martha. Jake is safe for now. We will leave him with Edith and Jonah for a while and see what develops. Maybe thee should go up to bed. Thee must be tired out from all this excitement."

Martha kissed her mama and papa on their cheeks and climbed the steep stairs to her and Jake's room. Without undressing, she burrowed under her blankets and trembled herself to sleep, admitting to herself that she greatly missed her brother's small warm body and cold feet.

Two weeks later, after the New Year brought in 1854, Jake came home.

"I had the best time, Mattie, 'specially since I didn't have to go to school."

"Well, you do now," she said. "So get ready."

Moments after Martha had spoken, an official marshal from Windham County appeared at the farm. She looked on in horror as he issued his orders.

"I'm sorry, folks," he said, "but the federal commissioner has called for you to appear in the Windham County Courthouse in Brooklyn for a hearing concerning your boy Jake here and Mr. Robert Dawes's claim under the Fugitive Slave Law that he's his slave. We have to take the child with us now. The hearing's scheduled for this afternoon."

"That is outrageous," Martha's papa responded.

"That may be so, sir, but the law is the law."

"What's he talking about, Papa?" Martha asked.

"There are now special courts to hear the Fugitive Slave Law cases."

"Can we refuse to go?"

"I'm afraid not. But, sir," he addressed the marshal, "don't we have time to seek legal counsel?"

"Nope. Seems this is a rushed case." The marshal then lowered his voice to a whisper. "Money talks, you understand."

Martha rushed to her papa's side as his face turned a bright red and his fists clenched.

"Let me go with Jake, Papa. I'll take good care of

him. He'll be frightened and confused to go off with strangers. And, you know, he might act poorly."

The marshal nodded his head. "Good idea, and you and your wife can follow in your buckboard."

Once Martha and Jake were in the marshal's carriage, Jake turned to her in great agitation.

"Mattie, where are we going?"

She tried to soothe him. "We have to go to Brooklyn. You've never been there, so it'll be exciting, don't you think?"

"But *why*, Mattie?" he demanded to know. "And why aren't Mama and Papa taking us? Who are these men?"

Martha did not think it was her place to tell Jake the truth. In fact, she had no idea how she would ever be able to do it anyway. His past was so complicated. And would he even understand her if she did try? Wasn't this something her parents should reveal to him? But she had to tell him something, because he was growing more fretful by the minute.

"There appears to be some confusion, Jake. This Mr. Dawes seems to think you are a child he lost a long time ago. So we have to go to the Brooklyn Courthouse so a judge can tell him he's made a mistake."

Jake looked even more puzzled. "What if the judge says I'm the child he lost?"

"That's ridiculous, Jakey. Of course no such thing can happen."

But Martha knew that it could. Again she recalled Adam Burke's words the day she first heard about the Fugitive Slave Law: "It's a bad day for us all."

The six-mile ride from Liberty Falls to Brooklyn went quicker than Martha had expected. Although the dirt road was rutted and in parts icy from the winter weather, it was well traveled and therefore in better shape than the smaller country roads were.

When they reached the Brooklyn village green, Martha immediately identified the intimidating court-house. It was bigger than any building she had ever seen. Bigger than the Unitarian church or the Quaker meeting house. She strained her neck to look up past the two floors to the cupola way on top with its weather vane pointing northwest.

Before she could count all its windows, Adam Burke rushed up to them. "Micah. Sarah. Martha. Jake. This is Matthew Prescott, a lawyer I've brought to help thee. I sensed the trouble ahead and called on him as soon as I heard about today's hearing."

Her papa stepped forward to shake both men's hands. "Thank you so much, Adam. Mr. Prescott. Have others heard? Will there be a crowd here?"

"No," Adam Burke said. "Everything happened too quickly. I'm afraid we're on our own."

Martha then saw Adam Burke hand her papa a paper and say softly, "Here are Jake's birth documents. See," he pointed, "they say he was born on October 11, 1846, in Torrington, Connecticut. The mother, Nora Jackson, died in childbirth. The father, Nathaniel Jackson, was also recently deceased."

"But, Adam," her papa started.

"Say nothing, Micah. Matthew will handle everything."

Her papa took the phony documents and walked over to her mama. As he whispered in her ear, Martha's mama covered her mouth with her two hands and nodded.

At that moment, Martha took Jake's hand and followed Matthew Prescott, an elderly, kind-looking gentleman, to a large oak table in the main hearing room. What, she wondered, would be Jake's fate? Surely a federal commissioner would find that Robert Dawes's claim was unfounded. Or would he? For at that moment, she heard Adam Burke tell her papa, "The law says that the judge will receive ten dollars for every person he returns to slavery, but only five for those he doesn't. Let's hope we get a fair hearing."

Martha held tighter on to Jake's hand than she ever had before.

"Let go, Mattie," he complained. "You're squeezing me too hard."

She loosened her grip just a bit, but she could feel Jake's restlessness increase, and she did not want him to misbehave in front of the officials. "Behave yourself, Jake. It's very, very important that you not cause a ruckus."

"Yes, Mattie. I'll try."

At five minutes before the hour of ten, Robert Dawes entered the court. He looked striking in his tan breeches and matching jacket. Martha distrusted the concerned look on his face as he stopped by Jake's side to gently, but authoritatively, pat his back. Jake shivered at the stranger's touch, and as if by instinct, Martha wiped away Dawes's touch with one of her own. In turn, she felt Jake relax.

The federal commissioner in this case was Judge Jeremiah Mason. Adam Burke whispered to the air that he was known for his keen mind, impartial rulings, and private abolitionist leanings. At ten o'clock on the dot, Judge Mason, his black judge's robe swaying side to side as he climbed up the steps to his bench, rapped his gavel on its wooden block, and bellowed so that his voice echoed in the near-empty room. "We all know why we are here but please state your claim, Mr. Dawes."

"In regard to the Fugitive Slave Law of four years ago, Your Honor," he responded, "I have documents here showing my ownership of this boy's mother and proving that she was with child when she ran away. You can see the dates here." He showed the judge a section of the papers in his hand. "And here," he pointed again. "According to our Maryland laws, any child whose parent is a slave is also a slave. Therefore, the boy is mine."

Jake jumped up. "Mattie," he cried out loudly, "is Mama a slave? And me, too? Are you, Mattie?"

Martha pushed him down with a thud. "No, Jake, I told you, this man is mistaking you for someone else."

But Jake could not be still. Although Martha tried with all her might to hold him down, he spun around to look at their mama, great bewilderment covering his face. It took several minutes before she could turn him around to face the patient, but puzzled, judge. Meanwhile, she could feel Jake's little bottom and legs moving up and down to a steady anxious beat. She touched his legs. He stopped for a minute, then began his movement once again. She gave up and turned her attention to the proceedings.

"We, however, are not in Maryland, Mr. Dawes," the judge thundered. "In any case, Mr. Prescott, do you have the boy's documents?"

"I do, Your Honor." Prescott took the papers that Martha's papa handed to him and approached the judge.

He studied them carefully and looked knowingly at Prescott. "These seem in order," Judge Mason noted. "The boy was born in Connecticut of local parentage."

Dawes interceded. "May I see them, Your Honor?"

"I don't think that is necessary or appropriate, Mr. Dawes. And in any case, sir, you should know that any child born on our land, even *if* his *supposed* mother was a fugitive slave, is by the law of 1848, banning slavery in this state, *forever* free." Martha liked how he emphasized the word "forever."

"I beg to differ with you, Your Honor," Dawes broke in.

"As you wish," insisted the judge, "but, Mr. Dawes, where is this woman you claim to be this boy's mother? I see his mother sitting right over there, and she does not appear to be anywhere near a slave or even an African to me." Even the judge, it seemed to Martha, participated in lying, just like everyone else, except, perhaps, for Robert Dawes.

Dawes stretched to his full height. "I don't know where the mother is. But the boy is hers. And, Your Honor, I might add, mine as well. Those documents must be falsified. I insist on seeing them."

Martha gasped. Was Robert Dawes claiming to be Jake's birth father? Martha had read about the terrible violence of slave owners against female slaves and about the many slave children that resulted from that violence. But, still, to hear it said firsthand in such a casual manner startled her and made her fear this man even more than she already did. The force of Dawes's claim made her take a sideways glance at her brother. Could his black curly hair and sharp chin come from Dawes?

The judge continued, "If you wish to view these papers, Mr. Dawes, I recommend you obtain a solicitor to help you out. In addition, do you have proof of your alleged paternity? Are you married to this boy's alleged mother and do you have proof of such a union? If not, this court sees no reason to hear any more of your thinly disguised hoax."

"Of course I have no such documents, Your Honor. I have a wife and children at home. This was something, ummm, extra, shall we say? We don't record such things officially. Surely, you must have some knowledge of our customs."

Judge Mason gave Robert Dawes a disgusted look.

"Mr. Dawes. I repeat. You have no claim here. No papers. No woman that I can see to claim to be Jake's mother, except Sarah Bartlett there, and I believe she has never been south of Connecticut. Is that correct, Friend Sarah?"

"Yes, Judge Mason," Sarah muttered timidly from her seat.

"Therefore, the case is closed. You have been mistaken, Mr. Dawes. Have a pleasant journey back to Maryland." And with those words, he was about to slam his gavel down when he paused. "And Mr. Dawes. A word of advice. Members of the Connecticut State Assembly are currently discussing a new law they will hopefully pass promptly. It will impose a five thousand dollar fine and five years' imprisonment on anyone who falsely swears that any free Negro is a fugitive slave. So just in case you try to bring a different case to this court, take heed."

With that, Judge Mason slammed down his gavel,

declared the hearing closed, and dismissed the court. Robert Dawes stormed down the aisle and out of the courtroom, but not before stopping before Martha's mama and papa.

"This is not done," he muttered just loud enough for Martha to hear. "I will have what is mine!"

"See, Jake?" Martha said, diverting Jake's attention away from Dawes, whom he was staring at with his mouth wide open. "I told you that this was all a big mistake. Let's go home with Mama and Papa."

"Mattie, I need to relieve myself really badly," he whimpered after Dawes was gone.

Martha hesitated, but since she, too, needed to use the privy, she took his hand, told her parents where she was going, and exited the courtroom, being careful to look up and down the main corridor to make sure that Robert Dawes was not still on the premises.

Once outside, she looked up and down the main street as well. All appeared quiet. She then led Jake around to the back of the building, being careful that he not wander off the narrow path into the deep snow on either side. Holding open the door to the smelly outhouse, she ordered, "Be quick, Jakey."

Jake made a face at her and entered the privy. As she waited for him to finish, Martha shook with cold, fear, and the need to use the outhouse, but she remained alert for any sound of a person walking around. All remained completely still. As Jake reappeared, she said, "Wait right here for me, Jake. I need to use the privy, too. I'll just be a minute. Don't move, hear?"

"Yes, Mattie," he answered.

Martha entered the privy. Her hands shook so that it

took forever for her to lift her skirt and undergarments and lower her pantalettes. And equally long to do her business and set her clothing right. When she was done and came back outside, there was no Jake. Frantic, she ran around front to the courthouse door calling his name. Only then did she see Robert Dawes's phaeton accompanied by his two henchmen on horses speeding down the road. Jake's face appeared for a moment in the rear window and then was gone. Martha ran after them as fast as she could, shouting for them to stop, but the phaeton, its occupants, and the two slave catchers disappeared from sight before she even reached the end of the Brooklyn village green. Out of breath and sobbing, she struggled back to the courthouse before collapsing in a heap.

CHAPTER 7

MARTHA LAY face down on the ice-covered path in front of the courthouse, where she had fainted. Her body shivered violently from the cold.

"Martha," her mama called, shaking her by the shoulders. "Martha. What happened? Where is Jake?"

Martha did not open her eyes until her papa sat her up and shouted at her as if she were deaf, "Where is your brother, Mahthah? Come on. Talk to me!"

"Dawes," she managed to whisper. "Dawes took him. I tried to stop him, Papa. I really did. But he got away."

As she began to cry, Adam Burke approached.

"Thee take Martha home quickly, Micah, just in case there's some danger here for her. I'll send the alarm out through the Anti-Slavery Societies, and I'll alert the New London and Providence Vigilance Committees to be on the lookout for him."

"Where does thee think he will go?" her mama asked.

"He must be planning to leave by ship, I would think," Adam responded. "Going overland to

Worcester or Boston or using some of the railroad lines would be too slow and too noticeable. My best guess would be to look to the ports."

Martha's mind was racing. She wanted to ask questions, but her mouth would not form any words. She felt weak and delirious. How would she ever be able to cope with her guilt? It was she and she alone who was to blame for Jake's kidnapping. As she started to lose consciousness again, she heard her papa's voice shaking with anger. "The scoundrels must've attacked my poor girl."

"Take her home, Micah," Adam insisted. "Call Dr. Wisch while I begin the search."

Martha's papa flinched. "Jake must be terrified. *I'm* terrified, and he's just a little boy and not as worldly as other boys his age."

Adam Burke hurried off to his buckboard as Martha's mama and papa helped her up onto theirs. About two hours later, she was home in her bed when her mama led Dr. Wisch into her room. She was barely cognizant, but she recognized him immediately. This was a man she positively did *not* like. He was loud and boisterous and poked and jabbed her in places where she did not welcome his touch. She recoiled as he approached her, his stale breath just an inch from her nose.

"Well, what have we got here?" he said as if he were at a town fair. "Martha, are you feeling ill?"

Martha refused to respond and simply glared at him, so her mama spoke for her. "Martha was attacked by slave catchers and cannot speak. We need her to do so, so she can help us know what happened to her brother Jake."

"Well, in cases like this, Friend Sarah, I believe

bloodletting would be most effective," Dr. Wisch said, opening his medicine bag. "Martha, now listen carefully, please. I have a jar of leeches here. I'll place them on your arms and chest and we'll bleed you so that bad elements are removed and you'll feel better and be able to help your mama and papa."

Martha trembled. She peered over her blankets at the slimy, black worm-like things and tears welled up in her eyes. She wanted to talk, but she just could not. Surely, her mama would not allow this man to proceed with his treatment. But she did, saying, "This will help thee, Martha, but be brave. I am here with thee."

Martha gripped her quilts with both hands, but Dr. Wisch was stronger, and pulled them away from her body. He then opened the jar, took out one of the odious creatures, and placed it on Martha's arm. She winced. He then took another one and placed it a short distance from the first. As the leeches sucked at her, Martha could no longer remain silent. She screamed, "Get them off me. Mama, help me," and slapped at her arms, managing to squish one of them and cause a bloody mess. Her mama put her hands over her ears and ran from the room.

At this moment, Martha was relieved to see her papa enter and quickly take in the scene. Surely, *he* would not allow this man to mistreat her. This she knew for certain, and she was right. Her papa immediately stopped the medical procedure. "Doctor, this is not helping our Mahtah. She's hysterical with fear. Please remove the leeches immediately."

"But, Mr. Bartlett," the haughty man responded,

"these'll help your daughter by removing the evil elements that have locked her jaw."

"I think, then, you have succeeded," he said as Martha screamed.

The physician reluctantly followed her papa's orders, packed his bag, and harrumphed as he left the room. For the rest of the day, Martha drifted in and out of consciousness. She felt feverish and achy from her fall to the ground when she fainted. Although at times she wanted to jump out of bed to go in search of Jake, her sense of shame and loss crippled her. At those moments, all she desired was to huddle under her quilts and block out everything that had happened. Her heartache was too much for her to bear. To ease it, she mumbled Jake's name and "It's all my fault" over and over again.

When she was awake, she constantly asked her mama or papa, "Has Jake come home yet? I want to see him."

All they could say was that they were awaiting news of him. There were search parties all over the state seeking information on his whereabouts.

The next day, Martha saw her aunt Edith's friendly face beaming down at her. "Come on, Martha, my dear. It's time you arose from your bed and helped your mama with her chores. It'll make you feel better, and she desperately needs your help."

Martha looked pitifully at her aunt, then pulled her quilts up over her head. "I can't, Aunt Edith. I just can't." It wasn't that Martha could not help her mama. She wanted to very much, but she simply could not get her body to work.

"We need to get you back into action, dear heart. Mary Rogers just arrived. Perhaps she can help you."

Mary Rogers, the woman who had nursed Jake when he was an infant, entered the room soon after. Martha liked her warm and nurturing presence but had no appetite for the herbal remedies she offered every time Martha or Jake was sick. Nonetheless, she allowed Mary to gently lift her to a sitting position against her pillows and then accepted her liquid mixture.

"Here, Martha. Drink this. I've made it especially for you. It has several herbs and plants in it . . . St. John's wort, rose hips, gingko, garlic, ginger, and a hint of mint."

Martha took one whiff of the mixture and promptly vomited. That was the end of that.

While her mama and aunt cleaned her up, her aunt Edith said, "I've heard that cold water baths every morning are most healthy and invigorating. Maybe, Sarah, if we gave Martha a cold water bath, it would provide her with the energy to get on her feet and back to her normal, active life."

"I am not sure about that," offered her mama. "It is so very cold outside, Edith. Maybe exposing her to cold water will make her ill."

"Please, Sarah," Aunt Edith said. "Let's try."

The two women left the room and soon after Martha heard the clatter of water being poured into the tin tub in the kitchen. When the noise ceased, her aunt and papa came upstairs.

"We're going downstairs to the kitchen," they insisted, "so you can have a nice cold soak. It'll make you feel better."

By now, Martha really wanted to get on her feet.

Her mind was clearing, but something in her spirit had been damaged, making for a debilitating melancholia. So she allowed her aunt and papa to help her down the stairs, where her mama, lost in her own fog, silently awaited.

"Ah, Martha," she jolted awake. "Let's give thee a nice cold bath."

Her papa left while her mama and aunt helped Martha to undress and then slid her body into the ice-cold water. In a second, she sprang up and yelled, "No! No! No!" Grabbing a nearby sheet from the laundry pile, she wrapped it around her body, ran upstairs, and dove into her bed. But the shock of the cold water had done its job. Martha's body was coming back to life.

As she sat rubbing her legs and arms vigorously to warm them up before getting dressed, her mama came storming into her room.

"Martha, this is no good," she raged as Martha had never heard her before. "I cannot tolerate this behavior any longer. Having Jake gone is woeful enough. How can we concentrate on finding him and bringing him home if thee continues like this? I need thy help with the household chores, and I need to stop worrying about thee."

Martha looked at her mama with her own anger and despair. "Jake. It's always been about Jake," she said in a low, angry voice, which grew louder as she continued. "Everything is about Jake. Jake. Jake. Jake. What about me? What about how I feel?"

Her mama gasped. "Thee selfish child," she chided. "Of course everything is about Jake. He has been kidnapped. Thee is safe."

Now that her tirade had begun, Martha could not stop it. Resentment of all the years of taking care of Jake, of guarding him, of doing so many chores around the house burst out of her.

"You don't understand, Mama. Everything has *always* been about Jake."

Her mama started to cry. Martha, confused and contrite, tried to comfort her, but her tears would not stop. "I know I have not been a good mama to thee or to Jake. The lies. The fear. I do not have the strength to bear them."

Martha pushed the quilts away, grabbed hold of the now damp sheet around her body, and knelt beside her mama. "Mama, please. I'm so sorry."

The two cried together until Martha heard the sound of feet rushing up the stairs. Hoping there was news of Jake, she released her mama and ran to the door. But there was no news. It was, instead, Becky.

"Martha. I've been longing to see you . . . Oh, I'm sorry." She paused. "I'll come back later."

Martha gave her friend a grateful look. "No, it's fine. Come on in."

Her mama, who had been wiping her eyes, got up, gathered herself, and left the room. Martha, embarrassed by her sheet wrapping, climbed back into bed.

"Is she all right, Martha?"

"No. None of us is, Becky."

"I've been so worried about you."

"I've been a bit ill," Martha responded, "but I'm getting stronger."

"What *happened*, Martha? The town is full of rumors. Did those wicked slave catchers hurt you?"

Martha could not deny her need to confess the truth. She was so, so tired of lies. Look how much trouble they caused.

"I'm so ashamed of what's happened to Jake, Becky," she said at long last. "It's all my fault that he was taken, you know."

"Psshaw, Martha. You've nothing to be ashamed of. You're just a thirteen-year-old girl. Well, thirteen and a half. Of course, you don't look weak and fragile, but, still, you couldn't fight off a band of slave catchers."

"You don't understand, Becky. I left Jake alone for a few moments to use the privy, and that's when they took him."

Martha took in a deep breath, so relieved she had finally told someone what had really occurred. She knew from overhearing her parents that they believed the slave catchers had hit her over the head and stolen Jake. They had never realized they had found her lying on the ground because she had fainted.

"Please don't tell my parents," she pleaded. "They still don't know the circumstances. I haven't told this to anyone before now."

Martha was shocked because Becky looked like she was going to laugh.

"What's so funny?"

"Of course, I'll keep your secret," she gulped, "but, Martha, what else could you have done? I mean, when a person has to use the privy, they must tend to that." Then she cracked a smile, and even Martha had to stifle a little laugh. She, of course, immediately stopped. It was not right to laugh at such a serious matter, she thought.

"But, Becky, everyone in the town must be blaming me for what happened. I'm too ashamed to face them. People will say mean things, and the children at the school will shun me."

"Are you serious?"

"Yes."

"Martha. People admire you."

"What do you mean?"

"Here you are, not quite an adult. Yet, as we all know, from since you were just six, you've been doing a *lot* of the work taking care of Jake. You showed how much you really love him, even if he is so difficult at times."

"I did?"

"Of course. Everyone is saying how brave you were down in Brooklyn."

Martha blinked. She was proud that people saw how much care she had given Jake, but she did not believe she had actually shown him love.

"All the children and the adults, too, are praising you and praying for you. They're all talking about that wicked Mr. Dawes and have even said that if he should ever come to Liberty Falls again, they'll lynch him."

Martha's jaw dropped.

"Becky, lynching is against the law. And many of the people in our town are Quakers. They don't believe in violence."

"Well, maybe not the Quakers. But lots of folk are grumbling."

Martha stared at Becky and remembered her gentle papa's clenched fists the first time Dawes confronted him.

"Are you sure, Becky?" she asked. "You know. About

people being proud of me. You're not just saying what my parents asked you to say?"

"I'm sure, Martha." Becky paused for a moment. "So? Are you gonna stay in bed and sulk over one mistake?"

"It was more than a little mistake, Becky. Don't you agree?"

"Maybe. But you can't stay in bed forever. So, are you gonna get moving or not?"

"I think it's time I get moving."

Martha had been ill for two whole days, and she still did not feel quite right. To get back to normal life would take a bit of effort. Silence prevailed for several more minutes as she gave the idea some thought.

At long last, Becky asked, "Are you wondering about Caleb?"

"Yes," Martha said, barely above a whisper. "How is he?"

"He's just fine. Working with your papa as usual. Wondering how you are and worrying about you *a lot*. He's been wanting to see you, but, you know, Martha, it wouldn't be proper for him, being a boy you know, to visit your bedroom. You're gonna have to get up and go see him. That is, *if* you ever wanna see him again."

"Are you sure he wants to see me?"

"Oh, Martha, don't be such a dolt!"

"He's not ashamed of me?"

Becky let out an exasperated sigh. "Martha Bartlett. You have to be the most ignorant girl in the whole of Liberty Falls. C'mon. Get. Up."

Martha slowly pushed her quilts off her body until Becky gave them one huge tug and they fell to the floor. Martha laughed. It felt so good.

"And maybe, Martha? Before you see Caleb? Or anyone? Maybe you should put on some clothes and comb your hair."

And with that, Becky gave Martha a big hug and ran out of the room, calling behind her, "See you soon, I hope. I've missed you."

After Becky left, Martha got up, put on a dress, and combed and plaited her hair. Using the bowl and pitcher of water on her chest of drawers, she took a washrag and wiped around her face. Finally, she put on her stockings and shoes and slowly edged her way down the stairs. Her parents and aunt were elated to see her.

"Mama. Papa. I'm ready to face the world, but not all at one time. If you don't mind, I'll just do my chores for a few days. I'm not ready to go to town or back to school."

"That's fine, Martha. One step at a time," her mama said.

"Is Caleb in the woodshop, Papa?"

"Yes, he is."

"Would you mind very much if I went to see him for a few minutes?"

"Not at all, Mahtah. Tell him I'll bring luncheon in a little while."

"Thank you, Papa."

Martha opened the door to the back of the house. It was freezing, and she could see a new blanket of snow on the ground. She ducked back inside for a shawl and then quickly walked to the woodshop.

The roaring blaze in the fireplace that greeted her felt wonderful. Caleb, whose back was to her, was sawing a piece of wood for a table he was making.

"Caleb?" she said softly.

At the sound of her voice, he spun around. Seeing she was alone, he rushed to her and embraced her, holding her close for several moments as he touched her hair and kissed her forehead.

"Are you all right, Martha?"

"Not really. But Becky just visited me and has made me feel much better."

"I've been so worried about you," he said with great concern. "I asked your folks if I could talk to you, but they said it wasn't proper for me to see you upstairs and that you couldn't come down. Did those slave catchers harm you?"

"No, Caleb. They never touched me. And anyway, it's all my fault that they took Jake."

"How can it be your fault, Martha?"

"I made it easy for them, Caleb. I took my eyes from Jake for just a few moments to use the privy. But it took too long with all my winter overgarments and my girls' clothing. I didn't think they were still around or I would've held in my needs. Please, Caleb, don't tell my parents. Becky knows and you know, but I don't want anyone else to know."

"Martha, you couldn't know they were still lurking around on the grounds. And you can't torture yourself like this. You must get on with your life. I promise to keep your secret, though I think it might be better for you to tell your parents. They've been sick with worry about you, not to mention their despair over Jake."

"I can't tell them. I'm humiliated and overwrought. If they knew that I had neglected Jake even for a moment, they would never forgive me. Caleb, that one moment,

the only time I was ever careless, was the time it mat-
tered the most. Now who knows what's become of Jake?"

"The Anti-Slavery Societies and Vigilance
Committees are searching for news of him, Martha.
They have eyes and ears all over the North *and* the
South. I'm sure they'll find him. Most likely, Dawes is
on his way to his plantation, and your parents or Adam
Burke will be able to go and get him."

"How? Dawes claims fatherhood. And once in
Maryland, Dawes will claim ownership as well."

"But he has no proof," Caleb said excitedly.
Apparently, he had given the situation a great deal of
thought while she had been wasting precious time in
bed. "*You* know that Jake's birth mother was a slave,
right? But even you don't know who his father was.
Dawes can't be sure that Jake's mother was the same
woman he's searching for because she's nowhere to be
found. Correct?"

"Yes."

"And he can't be sure he's Jake's father, either,
because there's no Mariah around to say so."

Martha followed Caleb with her eyes as he paced
around the workshop, his enthusiasm multiplying
with each sentence. "And, Martha, you don't know for
sure if the slave woman your father buried was even
this Mariah. She could've been someone else entirely.
Maybe Dawes was searching for some other woman.
Do you understand what I'm saying, Martha?"

Martha thought long and hard about what she was
hearing. Caleb made sense to her. If Dawes really
had no legal claim to Jake, why couldn't her family
hire some lawyers, go to Maryland, and bring him

back? After all, hadn't Dawes openly kidnapped a free Northern child?

"You're so brilliant, Caleb." She threw her arms around his neck and planted a big kiss on his lips. Then she blushed a bright red.

Still holding on to Caleb, Martha started thinking. Now was the time for her to stop acting like a child. Now was the time for her to become a woman, like the great abolitionists Lucretia Mott and Abby Kelley or, even better, the slave rescuer Harriet Tubman. Yes, now was the time for her to plan, push ahead, and seek information. She had lost Jake. Now, she would find him.

CHAPTER

OR THE next week, Martha concentrated on getting back her strength and resuming her normal routine. But there was no "normal" without Jake. The house was too quiet without his contagious laugh and high-energy antics. Her papa worked in his shop long hours and seemed reluctant to sit at the table or in the parlor with her and her mama. To Martha it seemed as if he felt guilty for not being a responsible head of his family. Her mama drew further into her shell. She cooked and knitted and even conversed a bit, but mostly when Martha sought her out she found her sitting in her rocking chair staring out the window as if waiting for Jake. There was no cheer in the home, just a longing for news of their lost boy.

Martha stayed at home, doing more than her share of the chores. In her spare time, she read any and all abolitionist books and newspapers that came into the house. She no longer lingered over the notices of kidnappings, however. Instead, she read about slave rescues.

"Caleb," she said one day after a month of interminable

waiting, "have you ever heard of the rescues of Shadrach Minkins in Boston and Jerry in Syracuse?"

"Can't say that I have."

"They were taken under the Fugitive Slave Law, just like Jake. But then mobs of people rescued them and whisked them away to Canada."

"That's interesting, Martha. But what does that have to do with Jake? He's probably already on Dawes's plantation."

"Well, I've been reading, and there are some brave people going down South to rescue loved ones who were sent there."

"Truly?" Caleb cut a slice of cheese from their luncheon and offered it to her. As she held it in her hand, she continued. "Of course, slave rescuers can't reveal any details. No names. No routes."

He gave Martha a meaningful look. "You mean like the Underground Railroad."

"Well, more than that. I've heard tell that Harriet Tubman has gone to the exact same area of Maryland that Jake might be in and helped bring her family members to freedom. It vexes the authorities that so many slaves are going missing."

"Sounds dangerous to me."

"Oh, it is. If they're caught, they get arrested. The Africs get sold way down South and the whites go to jail for a very long time."

Caleb cut some bread and offered it to Martha. She shook her head no.

"I wonder, Caleb, if Harriet . . ."

Martha stopped in the middle of her sentence as Adam Burke's carryall sped up their road.

"I have news of Jake," he shouted as he jumped down to the ground and ran to the house. Martha and Caleb ran after him.

"Please, tell us, Mr. Burke," Martha urged. "Where's Jake? It's been a month since Robert Dawes took him."

"I don't know where he is at this very moment, Martha, but I do have some news."

Martha's face fell, but she listened intently as Adam Burke shared his information.

"First, I must tell thee that we have had abolitionists all over Connecticut asking questions about your boy. And then there is this." He handed a copy of *The Liberator* to Martha's papa. Her heart stopped as she peered over his shoulder at the title of the front-page article: "Slave Owner Kidnaps Connecticut Boy." This was a nightmare come to fruition. Martha's papa read the short piece aloud:

"On January fifteenth, Robert Dawes, a slave owner from LaGrange, Dorchester County, Maryland, kidnapped seven-and-a-half-year-old Jacob Bartlett after an unsuccessful attempt to claim him under the Fugitive Slave Law. Dawes said the boy was the son of his slave, Mariah, who ran away in the fall of 1846. However, there is no evidence that Mariah came through Connecticut or that she is the mother of young Jacob.

"The Vigilance Committees of Connecticut and the child's parents are searching frantically for him. Please contact Adam Burke in Liberty Falls, Windham County, Connecticut, if you have any information concerning this tragic situation."

Martha took the paper from her papa. "May I keep this, Mr. Burke?" she asked.

"Yes, of course, Martha."

"Thank you. But, please, do you have any more positive news?"

"Yes, I do," Adam Burke said. "We have two eyewitnesses who claim to have seen Dawes with Jake."

Martha held her breath as Adam Burke continued.

"The first person to notice something unusual was a woman at an inn south of here in Norwich."

"When was that?" asked her mama.

"The evening of the kidnapping."

"Dawes was traveling fast," her papa noted.

"Yes. The woman said that a phaeton with a tall gentleman and a child stopped by the inn. There were two ruffians with them. The gentleman asked the woman for some bread, meat, and ale, but said he wished to eat in his carriage. The woman noticed that he had a Southern accent."

Martha sensed Adam Burke's hesitation to go on. "What is it, Mr. Burke? What's the matter?"

"Prepare thyselves."

Everyone in the group took a deep breath as Adam Burke went on. "The woman told her son to go ask her husband to prepare the plate. Meanwhile, the gentleman, let's say Dawes, descended from the carriage to stretch his legs. When he opened the door, the woman noticed that the little boy inside had a big welt on one side of his face. It was an angry red as if the boy had been struck mighty hard. She also saw a rope tied around his waist and attached to a metal loop on the floor. The child looked angry and sorrowful."

Martha heard her mama sob and grabbed for her hand. "Oh, my poor child. No one has ever struck him

before. He was raised in a gentle home, Adam. No
violence."

"I know, Sarah. I know," he replied.

"Why didn't she call for help, Mr. Burke?" asked
Martha. "There was obviously something amiss."

"She did, Martha. She immediately ran into the inn with
the intention of sending her son for the local constable, but
Dawes, sensing the woman's alarm, forewent his victuals,
hurried to the phaeton, and took off at top speed."

Silence filled the room.

"Is there any more?" asked her papa.

"Yes. The next time anyone actually saw the party
was in New London. One of our associates working
on the docks saw the group, well, we assume it was the
same group, arrive by the dock where a large sloop
awaited. As soon as the crew saw the phaeton arrive,
they started raising the sails. A man, a child on a tether,
and two rough riders accompanying them quickly
boarded the ship, leaving the horses and carriage aban-
doned on the dock."

"And?"

"Immediately after, the ship set sail and headed east
out of the Long Island Sound toward the ocean."

"And?"

"And nothing else for now. We have a contact
who knows how to reach Harriet Tubman, who's
just returned from a visit, shall we say, to Dorchester
County, where Jake should be by now. Mrs. Tubman
says there's no sign of him."

Martha pondered this information and then started
thinking out loud. "Maybe it just takes a long time to
sail to Maryland. Or he's hiding somewhere with Jake

until things quiet down. Or something happened to the ship on its way. Could it be that, Mr. Burke? Could something bad have happened?"

"Don't think that way, Martha," her papa urged. "Adam, what's the plan now?"

"Well, folks, there's nothing much we can do for now but sit and wait. There's a contact in Dorchester, in fact, in LaGrange itself, who's asking questions. She must be very discreet, thee understands, so it may take us a while to learn what's happened. In the meantime, the abolitionists all through our state are collecting money to offer Dawes for our purchase of Jake."

Martha was perplexed. "Purchase? How can you purchase a free boy?"

"Thee all must try to understand," Adam Burke said. "We know that we'll be offering a bribe, or a ransom, if thee prefers, for the boy. But, remember, Dawes is a slave master. He believes he owns the child. So we'll simply call it a purchase price."

Martha persisted. "But isn't that lying, Mr. Burke? It seems wrong to me to pretend to purchase him. Isn't that illegal here anyway? Buying a slave, I mean?"

"Martha, thee and thy parents of all people know that sometimes one has to lie or play a game in order to achieve freedom and justice. We shall play the slave owner's game. Now I must go. I'll be back as soon as I have more news."

Two whole months of anguish and torture passed without any word. At times, Martha felt such guilt and frustration that she dreamed of running away to Maryland to find Jake herself. But she had no idea how to do that. She was smart enough to know that she

really needed the help of the adults in the abolitionist community to save Jake. One young girl could not
take on such a monumental task all by herself, but she
was convinced that she could play a pivotal role in the
rescue. At long last, April, with its early signs of spring,
blossomed with news of Jake as well.

One evening, Adam Burke rushed to Martha's front
door and proclaimed, "Jake's at Dawes's LaGrange
plantation."

"Is this the truth? Has anyone actually seen him?"
asked Martha, elated that her brother was alive.

"Yes, Martha," he replied. "Our contact, a Mrs.
Perry, met Dawes's kitchen slave, Lucy, at the market in the town. She's known Lucy, who was born on
the plantation, all her life. She asked her about a new
slave child."

Martha held her breath. "She's seen Jake?"

"Lucy told Mrs. Perry that Robert Dawes returned
to the plantation after having been away for almost
three months. She said he looked travel weary, a bit
thin, even."

"He was probably worn out by Jake," Martha jested
in nervous relief. Her mama and papa stared at her in
shock.

Adam Burke continued, "She also said that he had a
child with him. He looked to be around seven or eight
years of age. Looked exactly like her daughter Mariah."

Martha gasped.

"Dawes told Lucy the child's name was Jake. Lucy
apparently begged him to let her take charge of the boy,
and he seemed relieved to comply. Said she should teach
him kitchen chores and keep him in her quarters."

Martha's mama held a handkerchief to her tearful eyes and asked, "Did this Lucy ask Jake about his mother?"

"She said the child was very quiet."

"Are you sure it's Jake?" Martha put in again. She seemed unable to hold her tongue.

"He told her his name was Jake. That he was taken from Connecticut. That his mama was Sarah and his papa Micah. And he demanded that Lucy call a constable to take him home."

"Ah," Martha laughed in relief. "That's Jake."

Even her mama and papa gave a little smile at her comment.

Adam Burke continued, "He told this Lucy that he knew nothing about anyone named Mariah. Of course, Lucy told Mrs. Perry that she was very worried about her daughter, who had run away about eight years ago. She had hoped she was safe in Canada or at least somewhere in the North, but now she feared that something evil had befallen her. She wants to know about her daughter as much as thee wants to know about Jake."

"This is so sad, Mr. Burke. Will you offer Mr. Dawes the ransom?" Martha asked.

"We're trying to arrange this now. I've written a letter that will offer him eight hundred dollars for Jake, but I'm waiting for one of our anti-slavery agents to carry it to Philadelphia, where it'll be carried on further south."

"Eight hundred dollars," Martha's papa mused. "That's a goodly sum. People have been so kind to us."

"Yes," Adam Burke agreed. "Let's hope that Robert

Dawes thinks so, too. He's a wealthy man, you know. Eight hundred dollars may seem a pittance."

"Mr. Burke," Martha added, "can Harriet Tubman help us if Mr. Dawes rejects our offer?"

"Let's try this approach first. If it doesn't work, we'll seek help elsewhere."

With that, Adam Burke left. Martha was elated by the news. Jake was not only alive, but apparently well. Now it would be a simple task of bribing the greedy slave owner and bringing Jake home. After all, now that he had experienced being with Jake, why would he want to keep him? He could hardly take care of himself, much less do the work of a slave. Maybe her parents and Adam Burke would allow her to be one of the party to go and get him. She was so curious to see what the South and its "peculiar institution" looked like.

Yet another very long but oddly hopeful month passed with no more word. Instead of fretting, however, Martha began planning. She hinted to Caleb that she wanted to go south herself for Jake's rescue, but he just looked at her as if she had lost her mind.

"Martha, be serious. You haven't been any further south than Brooklyn. Do you have any idea how to get to Maryland? Do you even have any money? And what about the impropriety of a girl traveling on her own?"

"But, Caleb, I would just be one of the rescuers, not the only one. Jake would be happy to see me, and I could help manage him."

"Well, aren't you the same girl who just a few months ago was afraid of even leaving this farm to go to town or school?"

"That was a different time, and no, I'm not the same

girl. I'm different. A lot's happened in a few months, and I've read a lot and learned a lot and planned a lot. I know I have to help Jake. He's my brother, after all. I neglected him, and I lost him. Guilt changes a person, you know. And besides," she added, "I was hoping that you might come with me."

"Are you jesting?" he asked. "Martha, first of all, I can't leave my family and my job here with your father. They all depend on me for money and help. Second of all, I'm not all that brave. I'm more of a stay-on-the-farm man. And third, I care for you too much to venture off on such a harebrained scheme. Let's leave Jake's rescue to those who have some expertise in such matters, shall we?"

Martha was greatly upset by Caleb's attitude. He sounded like an old man, not a young adventurous one. She had thought he would want to be part of the effort to save her brother from the worst evil of all—slavery. But after his initial anger at Jake's abduction, he appeared to minimize the seriousness of her brother's situation and just want to get on with life. She decided that for the present, the best approach was to agree with Caleb lest he mention something to her father.

"I see your point, Caleb. I'm too young and unknowledgeable to think about becoming a slave stealer."

For the next endless month Martha scoured all the books and newspapers she could find to learn something about Maryland. Maybe with more information, she could change Caleb's mind.

"Caleb," she said one Saturday during their usual luncheon together, "did you know that Maryland is actually not that very far south?"

"What do you mean?"

"Well, it borders Pennsylvania, you know."

"Really."

"Yes, on the north, and Delaware on the east."

"Delaware is slave, though, isn't it?"

"Yes," Martha said, "but it's small. And right across the Delaware Bay is New Jersey. And that's free."

"Martha," said Caleb.

"I'm just trying to learn about where Jake is," she hedged, "so that when someone with experience goes to get him, I'll know where they're going."

"Uh-huh."

In early June, Adam Burke returned to the farm. Martha greeted him eagerly.

"I need to speak to thy parents, and, of course, with thee as well, Martha." He looked so solemn that Martha immediately had misgivings.

"Please come inside. My mama's taken to her bed. This situation with Jake has broken her. But I'll ask her to come downstairs."

Once again Adam Burke brought the family both bad and hopeful news at the same time. With each word, Martha noted her mother drawing into herself, becoming more remote, sometimes simply staring into space.

"I've had a response from Robert Dawes," he told them. "He's refused our offer. Says he doesn't wish to sell the child to us. Says he's too valuable."

Martha drew in a deep breath. "What does that mean?"

"It means that he wishes to taunt us. Here, let me read part of the letter to thee. 'I wish to keep the boy for at least two years while he acclimates to his station in life. Then I may consider selling him. His fair looks and training as a house slave will make him very valuable.'"

Martha could not believe her ears. "He would sell a boy he claims to be his own son?"

"I believe he's saying this just to exert his authority over us. However, there are a number of slave owners who have sold their Afric children. And then there are some, I'm happy to say, who have actually freed them."

"But what about a lawyer, Mr. Burke?" asked Martha. "Can't we retrieve Jake by proving he was born here a free boy?"

"You know, Martha, that Jake's birth documents were falsely made. There's actually no proof he was born here. Dawes has shown his own solicitor documents proving ownership of Mariah. Apparently, Jake resembles his grandmother Lucy a great deal, and a Maryland judge will see this as proof of Dawes's ownership. Also, Dawes does claim paternity, and Maryland accepts his word on that. Custom, you know."

"So, what next?" asked Martha's papa.

Adam Burke paused. He looked at Martha as if he was very, very carefully considering his next words.

"I've heard from our contacts in Philadelphia who see Moses on a regular basis."

"Moses?" Martha asked.

"The slaves' secret name for Harriet Tubman," Adam Burke explained. "She said that she's willing to rescue Jake. She just needs a bit of time to make the arrangements."

"Perhaps," said Martha, "the slave woman Lucy can help her."

"At this point, we don't know."

Martha sat biting her lip. She knew what she wanted to say, needed to say, and she trembled at the thought of it.

"I want to go too," she stammered, "and bring Jake back."

Her mama immediately came out of her stupor. Martha was surprised that she had actually heard and comprehended the conversation. "That is impossible, Martha. Thee is too young and the trip is too arduous and too dangerous. I am sure that Mrs. Tubman would not agree to take thee with her."

Martha held her ground. "I'm almost fourteen. I've been reading all the newspapers and all about Maryland, and I'm certain I could get there on my own. I could meet Moses there. Mama, we raised Jake not to go with strangers. And after being kidnapped, don't you think he'd be even more frightened if someone else he didn't know tried to take him? Maybe he'd even fight them off." To seal her case, she added, "Also, you know he'll most likely be loudmouthed and difficult and confused and scared. But you know that once he sees me, he'll come willingly."

"No, Martha," her mama half sobbed. "Thee cannot go. I shall not risk losing thee as well as Jake."

"You won't, Mama. I'll be most careful."

Martha was persistent. She just had to show her parents the benefits of her plan.

"Look, Mama, I can go on a ship all the way from New London to Baltimore. Then I can hire a smaller boat to take me to LaGrange. See?" She took out a map she had in her pocket. "It's not really that far. And

Pennsylvania is right there, right across the border. And there're many abolitionists there. I'm sure they'll be waiting for us with open arms. It's not like going to the far South, like to Mississippi or Alabama or something."

Her mama just shook her head at her.

"But, listen, Mama. It'll be easy. I can find Jake through this Mrs. Perry and Lucy, talk to him, and then simply walk away with him. Then Mrs. Tubman can lead us by the Underground Railroad to Pennsylvania."

Her papa exploded. "Are you in your right mind? First, you are too young and inexperienced to go on your own. You've rarely been beyond Liberty Falls and never by yourself. Second, you're a girl. People will expect you to have a chaperone. If you don't, they'll find you suspicious. Third, it's far too precarious. So, no. I say no."

"Papa. Perhaps the Vigilance Committee can find me a chaperone to Baltimore. Once I get there, I can pretend I'm just a local girl going to visit an aunt. Is Mrs. Perry white or black, Mr. Burke?"

"She's black, Martha, but that's beside the point. I don't think thy idea is very realistic. Remember, Robert Dawes and both of his henchmen know what thee looks like. They'll recognize thee immediately."

"I could use some herb dyes to color my hair. Or I could wear a big bonnet that hides my face."

"Mahthah," her papa almost shouted. "Wake up. This is not like one of the stories you've read. This is real life."

While he spoke, her mama became more agitated.

Her cheeks were flushed bright pink and her eyes full of tears. Finally, words spilled out of her mouth.

"Martha, listen to us. It is too dangerous. Look at thy skin. It is tannish, and maybe someone will mistake thee for an Afric person."

Martha examined her arm and then saw her father cough and swipe his big checkered hanky across his eyes. She was startled, never having known her father to cry. Or to give her mama a hard look as he was doing now. Her mama promptly burst into uncontrollable tears.

"What's happening?" Martha cried out. "Why is my skin so important that you're both having fits of emotion? You've always said Jake and I have the same skin color and that's why people don't question his race. What's so different now?"

As she looked around wildly trying to figure out why they were so vexed, she felt her papa's strong arms encircle her as he kneeled down next to the stool she was perched upon. Slowly, she calmed down.

"It's time we told her, Sarah," he said while her mama simply nodded her head. Martha saw Adam Burke get up as if to leave.

"Stay, Adam. You know most of this anyway," her papa said. Adam Burke sat back down. Martha then learned another stunning secret that her parents had held for more than thirteen years.

"You see, Mahthah," her papa began in a voice so soft she had to strain to hear him, "your mama and I, well, for some reason we were never able to have a child."

"But you had me!!!" she responded.

"Shhhhh. Let me speak and then you can ask me whatever you want to know."

"Yes, Papa."

"Like I said, we tried hard for ten years to create a child, but fate was not on our side. Then one day, your mama went out to get the basket from the outside shed to gather eggs and there you were, a tiny newborn infant fast asleep."

"You're lying," she said. "This family always lies."

"No, I'm not. We should have told you long ago. But with Jake here . . . well, it became most complicated."

"So, who am *I* then?"

"You are Mahthah, our daughter."

"No. I mean, who *am* I?"

Her papa bit his lip, gave her a squeeze, took her hand, and said, "We don't know. When we found you, you were wrapped in a blanket that looked like it might have been made by one of the wandering Indians who sometimes come through the town poor and alone. We heard there was a young girl with child seen with a traveling peddler, one of those Southern European types or maybe a fugitive slave, but they were long gone. Your mama and I, we saw you as a gift from Heaven, and we claimed you as our own, just as we did Jake."

Martha was stunned. This made no sense, and yet it made perfect sense. She and Jake, both orphans. She looked again at her skin and then at her black plaits, which hung down from both sides of her head, and then at her mama's blonde hair and her papa's blue eyes.

"Why didn't anyone in town ever say anything? Everybody is always telling gossip."

"Because within a short time, everyone just put it out of their thoughts. Like with Jake. Eventually, they just forgot about it. And your mama and I were going to tell you when we thought you were mature enough to know. I guess we just didn't want that time to ever come. You see, for us, you *are* and always have been ours, connected by our hearts and souls."

Martha's mind was rushing. Thoughts flew in and out as she tried to comprehend the meaning of this huge revelation. "So, I'm just like Jake? Actually, worse? I'm a foundling?"

"Yes, a foundling. But not worse. Why would you think that?"

"Because you know who his parents are, but not mine. And my real mama might be an Indian and my papa colored of some kind?"

"Mahthah, understand this. We are your mama and papa, not anyone else. Although we're not sure of where you came from, it's no matter to us."

"But it is to me, and to who I am now in this world. Tell me what you know."

"We don't know who your mother or father were, and we have no way of finding out."

For several minutes, no one said anything. Martha's papa kept hold of her hand. Her mama stopped crying, knelt next to her, and held her other hand. Martha, meanwhile, stared into space, trying to absorb what she had just heard.

After several moments, Adam Burke said in a low, quiet voice, "I know this is a huge discovery for thee to take in, Martha. But, if we can return to the question of Jake for just a moment, I'd like to say that I think

Martha has just cause to want to help her brother. I can understand thy fears, but, on the other hand, I think we can come up with a good plan to ensure her safety. The way she looks might actually help in the rescue, as she can be taken for white or black. And it does seem true that Jake might resist going with people he doesn't know. Martha has always been such a responsible girl. Sometimes I think she is much more mature than many girls her age."

"I cannot accept this," Martha's mama said as she slowly rose from her knees and left the room. Her papa looked after her with great concern, but he remained where he was.

"I should be the one to go, not Mahthah," he said.

"But, Papa," she insisted, "you can't leave Mama alone. She needs you. And this is the busiest time of the year for your woodshop. Caleb can't handle that for you."

"I'm very fearful of the outcome, Mahthah," he replied. "I love you dearly, as does your mama. And we both love Jake equally. So this is an almost impossible decision for me. I couldn't bear it if I lost you, too."

"You won't lose me, Papa. I'll be very careful."

"I need to think about it. Adam," he added, "I'll get back to you when I decide what to do."

"Time is the one thing we don't have, Micah," Adam Burke said. "Mrs. Tubman is planning a rescue real soon, and after that, who knows when she'll go to Maryland again."

"Papa," Martha pleaded, "please. I need to help Jake."

Minutes that seemed like hours passed before Martha's father spoke again.

"Well, if Adam here thinks you might be essential to the rescue, even though I may live to regret it, I'll support your desire to go, especially since I can't. But, Adam, I need to know my Mahthah will be safe. You must promise me she will always be with an adult."

"I promise," Adam Burke replied.

"And she'll be kept away from Dawes and his men at all cost."

"Of course."

"And that Harriet Tubman herself will guide her and Jake home safely."

"Yes. Absolutely."

"And, Mahthah, promise me, you'll be mindful of everything Mr. Burke says and that you and Jake will both come home to us, your parents."

"I promise, Papa."

"Then I suppose I give my consent."

He hugged Martha tightly. "But I will not rest easy until you are home again."

Adam Burke rose from his chair. "I'll take my leave then, but I'll return soon. I'll pray for thee, all of thee."

After he left, Martha's papa went in search of her mama. Martha herself was too self-conscious of her new identity to rush to reveal it to Caleb, so she said nothing. But a few days later when Becky came by to knit, she thought she would see what would happen if she shared her secret. After all, weren't secrets by their very nature meant to be shared with a special few? Hadn't she seen the results of keeping everything to oneself?

"Becky," she said, "have you ever wondered what it'd be like to be someone else?"

Becky looked up in between stitches. "Like who?"

"I dunno. Like maybe an Italian or an Indian."

"What an amusing thought, Martha! I've heard that Eye-talians are infidels. They're Catholic, you know. Not Protestant, like us. And my mama and papa say that's bad. And we all know that Indians are uncivilized, so I don't think I'd want to be either of them."

Martha gulped at Becky's intolerance, but she continued anyway.

"How about being colored?"

Becky put her needles down. "Oh, no. I wouldn't like that at all. No one here would want to marry me. I think I like being just like I am. White. And Unitarian."

Martha squirmed in her seat and busied herself with the stitch she had dropped during her questioning. Maybe this was not the best time to tell Becky the truth about herself. She worried about what would happen to their friendship once the news of her parentage came out. And how Caleb would react, too.

Meanwhile, Adam Burke led the effort in hatching a plan that would protect Martha as best as anyone could but also rescue Jake. After several weeks, he arrived at the house to present the final details.

"This was not easy to arrange, Martha, so I pray it's successful. Many people are reluctant to include thee in Jake's rescue. Thee is so young and innocent of the world. But we have one chance to rescue Jake, and thee may very well be the key to our success."

"It'll work, Mr. Burke. I'm sure of it," Martha responded.

"Okay. This is the plan," he said. "Martha, thee'll travel south with Charles Murdoch, a member of the

Philadelphia Anti-Slavery Society, who is visiting family up in Worcester. He'll stop here on his way home to pick thee up. Thee'll travel in a variety of private conveyances to reach Philadelphia."

"Like what?" asked Martha.

"Well," Adam Burke responded, "a carriage to New London, then a sailing ship to New York and another to New Jersey, then another carriage to Philadelphia. From there, a Maryland abolitionist couple, Samuel and Caroline Smith, will accompany thee to Dorchester County via a small boat and yet another carriage. When thee arrives, thee'll be lodged with Lorraine Perry. Mrs. Perry and Harriet Tubman will figure out a way for thee to meet Jake, but thee will do so in their company. Thee will then head home with Mrs. Tubman through the Underground Railroad. I hope this is not too arduous for thee."

"Oh, no, Mr. Burke. It's all just fine," Martha responded.

In fact, she was feeling more excited by the minute. The adventure and danger were surprisingly appealing to her, she who had always been so shy. If the people of Liberty Falls admired her for having sheltered Jake for all these years, imagine how they would praise her when she brought him home!

Adam Burke interrupted her reverie and assured Martha's mama and papa, "Moses already has made a scheme to bring a few of her family members to freedom, and Martha and Jake will become part of that group." He added to Martha, "But this is truly dangerous business, Martha. Thee will be expected to obey all the people involved in this rescue, especially Mrs. Perry and Mrs. Tubman. Making thine own plans could result in tragedy for everyone. Does thee understand?"

"Of course, Mr. Burke. When do I leave? And how soon shall I return?"

"Thee will leave the day after tomorrow. The entire venture should take no more than two weeks."

Martha saw the look of dismay on her mama's face. "Don't worry, Mama. That's not such a long time. And think how happy you'll be when I come home with Jake by my side."

Adam Burke raised his thin body from the chair he was sitting in and got ready to leave. "There's still much for us to do. Charles Murdoch and I will come for thee at sunrise, Martha, the day after tomorrow."

"I'll be ready."

Martha walked Adam Burke out to his carryall and then ran to the woodshop to tell Caleb everything that had taken place. He was not happy with the plan, not with any of it, and he was both shocked and disturbed by the story of Martha's birth, which she had finally decided to reveal to him.

"My parents shouldn't have kept such important information about my past from me," she said.

Caleb was uncharacteristically silent as he continued working on the chair he was making.

"Caleb? I know you're upset about my going to the South, but I promise that I'll be careful."

"That's one thing, Martha, but not the only thing," he responded.

"What is it?" she asked.

"It's about the circumstances of your birth," he said.

"Don't worry. I'll adjust to it over time."

"But will I?" he asked softly.

"Caleb? Look at me. What are you saying?"

"I don't know, Martha. This is big news that you've just told me. Your not being white, or possibly not being white, or never being able to know if you're white, is a shock. It changes everything."

"Why?"

"Because I don't think I can see us together in the future if you're not white. I mean, I'd always be your friend, but . . ." His voice disappeared into silence.

"What are you saying?"

"Because if we had children, life would be very difficult for them. Isn't that one reason your parents kept your past a secret? If you and all the town accepted you as white, then no one would treat you differently or be hateful toward you."

Martha's head was spinning. "But I always thought you believed people were equal. I never thought you suffered from colorphobia. Look how you've always loved and protected Jake even after you heard he was black."

"You misunderstood, Martha. I've always believed that slavery is wrong. But I've never believed that blacks are equal to whites. It's just not so."

"But what makes today different from yesterday? How can I have been your equal then but not now?"

Caleb looked dismayed. "I dunno. I'm all confused. But that's just how it is. I don't believe the world is kind to marriage between the races and certainly not to any children of such a union."

"So you all of a sudden don't love me anymore? Just because none of us will ever be sure if I'm white or not?"

"Oh, I love you," he said, "but I'm not sure that I should."

Martha could not believe what Caleb was saying. When he turned his back to her, she ran out of the woodshop and into the house. Upstairs, she collapsed onto her bed, grabbing her rag doll to her heart.

"I'll show you, Caleb Franklin. I'm the same Martha. Well, no, I'm a different Martha. For one thing, I'm not so shy and quiet since Jake's gone missing. And for another, I may be white, or Indian, or black or maybe even all of them. And I'm gonna be a slave stealer and bring Jake home. And then see what you think of me!" And with those words, Martha sobbed herself to sleep.

CHAPTER

9

AT THE crack of dawn on the appointed day, Martha was ready and waiting for Adam Burke and Charles Murdoch. Her heart fluttered, beating out an internal rhythm: "I'm on my way. I'm on my way." She couldn't wait to leave to find Jake *and* to have an adventure.

"Now, Martha," her mama warned the night before as, with trembling hands, she gave Martha a rather small carpetbag, "thee must be able to carry the bag easily for long distances, so thee must not take heavy items."

Martha brought a change of clothing, all lightweight and gray so she would not be conspicuous. She also took her brush for her hair, which now hung down to the middle of her back. She would wear her sunbonnet but included in her bag a shawl even though it was well into June and the Chesapeake area should prove even hotter than New England.

Her mama spoke quickly in short gasps as if she had trouble breathing. "Thee will be traveling some by sea,

Martha, and it can get cool. And then there are evenings as well."

Her mind already on its way south, Martha listened with half an ear. "Yes, Mama.

Whatever you say."

At the last minute, Martha decided to place in her pocket one of the tiny carved horses her papa had made for Jake and the handkerchief Caleb had given her at the Anti-Slavery Fair.

Adam Burke and Charles Murdoch arrived in two carryalls around six o'clock. The sky was already bright with sunshine and Martha's mood reflected the happy feeling of the weather. Her mama handed her a sack filled with bread, cold meat, cheese, fruit, and a tin cup and hugged her so tightly that Martha had to struggle to free herself.

She was impatient to leave, but her papa took his time embracing her so hard she thought he would squeeze her to death.

"Take care of yourself, Mahtah. Be safe and careful. Please."

"I shall, Papa, and I'll see you in just a couple of weeks."

"Martha," Adam Burke reminded her as he helped her up onto the seat of the high carriage, "remember rule number one for thy work on the railroad. Do not . . . I repeat . . . do not act independently. Thee has always been an obedient girl. Now thee will be part of a very well-planned rescue that relies on everyone working together. Listen carefully to the people in charge. Do as they say without questioning them. They have great experience and know what they're doing."

"I shall, Mr. Burke. I promise."

As if as an afterthought, Adam Burke gave Martha an envelope. "And here are two sets of forged identity papers showing thee and Jake as free people."

Martha was surprised. "Why would we need these?"

"Because in the South, people may see thee as colored."

"In that case," she asked, puzzled, "how shall I act?"

"As thee does now, I'd imagine."

Martha quickly placed the envelope in her carpetbag. Looking up, she saw Becky running up their dirt road.

"Wait, Martha," she called. "I brought you some blackberry cakes for your journey."

Martha slid down awkwardly from her seat while Becky caught up with her.

"Caleb told me everything, Martha," she said, handing over the cakes. "Please be safe."

"I shall, Becky."

Martha embraced her friend and kissed her on the cheek. Becky whispered in her ear, "I love you, Martha, any way you are."

"And me you, Becky."

With some effort, Martha climbed back into the carriage, and the rescue began. A pang of anxiety swept over her as she saw her parents fade into figures smaller than ants and thoughts of Caleb's rejection thrummed through her heart. But then she grew excited. After all her reading and planning and begging, she was finally, truly, on her way to the South.

Once Liberty Falls was behind her, Martha took a careful look at her chaperone. Charles Murdoch was a quiet gentleman of about sixty with exceedingly fair skin, startling blue eyes, and a shock of white hair sticking out from beneath his hat. He was not talkative at all, so she decided to initiate a conversation.

"Thank you, Mr. Murdoch, for volunteering to accompany me to Philadelphia."

"My pleasure." Then silence.

This would be a long day, Martha thought. But at least his silence was not unfriendly.

"Ummm, Mr. Murdoch. Have you done much work for the Underground Railroad?"

The man's shoulders tensed.

"My dear girl," he said quietly. "An important rule for you to know is that you must never, and I mean never, ask anyone about the Underground Railroad."

So, thought Martha, this was rule number two, and she repeated it in her mind so she would not forget it. "Do not ask anyone about the Underground Railroad."

"Why not, Mr. Murdoch? You're obviously a friend of the slave or you wouldn't have offered to help me."

"This is so, but it's important for your safety, for mine, for the fugitives, and, well, for everyone involved, that the work remain secret and that only a very few people know the entire system. Do you understand?"

"Not exactly."

"The less each of us knows, the less chance that if caught, we can reveal knowledge to our opponents. So, you mustn't ask anyone questions. If you do, they'll feel unsafe. And you may very well put yourself in a dangerous position."

"I see." And she did, for hadn't she lived with that same secrecy her entire life?

For many miles, the two rode in a companionable silence. Martha observed the sights around her. The farms. The lessening of the hills. The trees and flowers and occasional deer as they loped across the road. After three hours of bumping along half in the shade of trees and half in the hot sun, the two stopped for luncheon by a spring with a little waterfall. Martha filled her cup with water, but Mr. Murdoch simply tilted his head, opened his mouth, and drank. He then splashed his face.

"Ahhhh. That feels good. Try it, Martha. It'll refresh you for the rest of today's journey."

Even though she did not want to get her dress wet, Martha allowed the cold spring water to splash over her face and neck. It sure did feel good.

The second half of the ride took place in the extreme heat of the day. As Martha swayed from side to side in the carryall, she nodded off. Twice she awoke to find herself leaning against Mr. Murdoch's arm. With great embarrassment, she apologized.

"Don't fret, Martha. I have three grown daughters and two sons and have experienced many a hot, sleepy head collapse on my arm when riding in the summer heat."

In the late afternoon, Charles Murdoch turned off the main thoroughfare onto a dirt road leading to a distant farmhouse. As they reached it, an extremely tall, lean woman with a huge white apron came out onto the wide porch to greet them. Mr. Murdoch introduced them.

"This is Martha Bartlett from up in Liberty Falls," he said. "She's on her way to visit her aunt in Philadelphia, so I've offered to accompany her. Martha, this is Suzanne Carpenter, my niece."

Ah, of course. The lies. But these were an essential part of Jake's rescue, so they were all right.

With a sense of relief and wonder Martha followed the tall Mrs. Carpenter into the cool and airy home. It had a parlor twice the size of hers and attached to the rear Martha could see a large kitchen. Her hostess took her directly to a bright bedroom on the first floor. "There's water in the jug for drinking, and some in the pitcher on the dresser for washing. After you've rested, perhaps you'd like to have a lemonade on the porch?"

"Yes, ma'am. I would . . . very much."

After Mrs. Carpenter left, Martha closed the door and dropped onto the soft down mattress and immediately drifted off to sleep. She dreamed that Jake was calling her. He faded in and out of her vision with the saddest look on his face that she had ever seen. When she awoke, she felt as if he was still with her, and it took a while for her to shake off his image.

In a dreamlike daze, Martha joined seven lively, talkative Carpenters for dinner. As they passed around plates of chicken, boiled potatoes, fresh peas, biscuits, and, for dessert, slices of warm strawberry-rhubarb pie, Martha remained silent except to answer an occasional question about her family and her town.

During dessert, the eldest son, Jed, asked, "Do you know much about the working of the Underground Railroad, Martha? I hear it's quite active up in your neck of the woods."

Unsure of what to say, Martha looked at Charles Murdoch, who gave her an almost imperceptible nod indicating she should say nothing.

"I'm sorry, Jed, but I don't know anything about it."

"I'm surprised," he returned. "I hear tell that lots of folks up that way are involved in it."

Martha simply smiled and shrugged her shoulders.

After sitting on the porch for a bit to watch a beautiful sunset, Martha said her good nights and went to bed. Again, she dreamed about Jake. This time he moved closer to her, his mouth wide open as if calling her name, but the rope tied around his waist stopped him from reaching her. She woke with a start. The sun was streaming through her window, and she quickly rose and got dressed.

"Mr. Murdoch," she asked as they once again headed south on the main road, "why did you stop me from answering Jed's question?"

"Ah, Martha. Another rule for working on the Underground Railroad. Never, and I mean never, answer any questions that would disclose information about anyone's work on the railroad."

So, rule number three, Martha thought. She sure hoped there would not be many more, or she might start to forget them.

"But why not?" she asked instead. "These were your family members, and I'm sure they can be trusted."

"So you would think, but I don't see them every day and I don't know what they all believe. Perhaps Jed doesn't support the work of the railroad. Perhaps he's simply seeking information to pass on to someone else. I wouldn't know that."

Martha sighed as she pondered all the lies and secrecy of the Underground Railroad. Were they really so very necessary? She longed for a more open life, one where she could say and do anything she wished without having to look over her shoulder all the time or be silenced by a non-trusting adult.

Again the day passed with an abundance of changing scenery. The land flattened, the vegetation changed to something she had never seen, and the breezes brought in a smell that she did not recognize. She turned her head into the wind and breathed deeply.

"You're getting a whiff of salty air and salt water, Martha. And you can see how there are plants that look sort of scrubby. See the long reeds over there?" She looked to where Mr. Murdoch pointed to tall grassy plants with puffs of brown grainy heads. "And if you listen real careful-like, you'll hear the sounds of the seagulls."

Martha cocked her head and soon heard a bird that sounded as if it were laughing.

"Is that it?"

"It sure is. And," he pointed, "you can just see the water of the Long Island Sound way out there in the distance."

Within a half hour, Martha spotted a bustling town on the water's edge with high sailing masts poking up toward the sky. She had never seen such a beautiful sight. Out on the blue water were a number of large ships with sails open full in the brisk breeze. Further out, she thought she saw a faint blue hilly piece of land.

"This is New London," Mr. Murdoch said. "See, way out there is Long Island. You can just make out the bluffs along the shoreline."

"It's beautiful," Martha sighed. "I've only seen drawings of these things in my books. It's so colorful, isn't it?"

"Yes, it is. And soon you'll be on that nice blue water. We'll be boarding a large sloop that a friend of mine owns. I often sail on it when I come to New England. It'll leave here for New York early in the morning."

"Will it take long to get there?"

"Maybe a day or two, depending on the wind. We'll go west," he pointed to his right, "on Long Island Sound, then around to the East River, and to New York." Then he added with some concern, "I hope you won't get seasick."

"I hope not. I've read that it's most unpleasant."

Turning his attention back to driving the carriage, Mr. Murdoch just smiled and nodded. Martha smiled, too. So far, being on the Underground Railroad was as easy as riding the buckboard into Liberty Falls. Or walking down the road to school when there were no slave catchers around. Why, it was even as easy as sitting by the brook dipping her feet into the cool, refreshing water. At this rate, she would be back home in no time. Once she reached LaGrange, she and Mrs. Tubman would simply walk up to Dawes's plantation, take Jake by the hand, and head home. Easy.

And, indeed, except for her dreams about Jake, the journey south continued to be uneventful. Her only fright came the first time the sailboat heeled, dipping one side close to the water, and she thought she would fall in. She grasped hold of the railing and asked in a shaking voice, "Mr. Murdoch, why is the boat tipping over? Will it turn upside down and drown us?"

"No, Martha," the kind man answered, "it leans with the wind, but the bottom is filled with ballast that keeps it afloat. Don't worry about it."

It took a while for Martha to relax and get her sea legs, but she did. Joyfully, she turned into the wind so the warm June breeze could wrap around her face, pushing her long plaits straight out behind her while the beautiful blue water occasionally splashed her. When in the late afternoon the wind died and the sails sagged, the captain anchored for the night. Martha went to sleep early and once again dreamed of Jake. This time he was in a sloop's cabin just like hers, but while she could leave hers at will, he was locked in. She dreamed that he pounded on the door and kicked it with his little legs, but in the end, he curled up on his bunk and cried himself to sleep. When she awoke, she was wet with sweat and sea dampness, and it took her some time to remember where she was.

As soon as she saw Mr. Murdoch the next morning, she asked, "Do you know much about spiritualism?"

"It's all the rage, isn't it, Martha?" he replied. "The Fox sisters have made it quite popular with their rappings and séances and communing with the dead. Why do you ask?"

"Ever since I left home, I've been having vivid dreams about Jake. I'm wondering if perhaps he's been trying to reach me," she responded.

"Well, spiritualists claim to communicate with the dead, Martha. Are you afraid something bad has happened to your brother?"

"I don't believe he's dead. What a horrible thought! But, can spiritualists hear from people who are alive?"

"I don't think so. It's probably just your nerves. Try not to fret about it. You'll soon be with him and then will know for sure how he is."

By midday the sloop reached the East River. As it came close to a wide harbor, Martha could see many buildings on each shore and crowded ferries hustling back and forth.

"I never imagined New York to be so huge, Mr. Murdoch," Martha said in wonder. "I wish I could stay here and see it all."

"No time for that, Martha. We'll be anchoring on the east side of the river and staying with a friend of mine in the town of Brooklyn for the night, and then we'll be on our way."

"Brooklyn?" gasped Martha. "Like in Connecticut?"

"Same name," Mr. Murdoch smiled, "but very different places."

Brooklyn, New York, was certainly bigger than Brooklyn, Connecticut. It was larger than any place Martha had ever seen. Once on land, she followed Mr. Murdoch up a steep hill to an area with many houses made of brown stone. Most were two or three stories high with windows facing the river and, to her surprise, each was attached to the ones next to it.

"This area is called Brooklyn Heights," he explained. "It has numerous abolitionists. Do you know of Henry Ward Beecher?"

"Yes, of course. He's Harriet Beecher Stowe's brother, isn't he?"

"Right. Well, his Plymouth Church is right down the street."

Martha strained her neck to try to see it, but Mr. Murdoch was anxious to arrive at his destination. Soon, he knocked on the door of a grand brownstone and was greeted by a woman in a plain black dress with a heavy accent that Martha did not recognize.

"Top o' the mornin'," she said with a big grin.

"And the rest of the day, too," responded Mr. Murdoch with a laugh.

"'Tis so good to see you, Mr. Murdoch. 'Tis been way too long a time that's passed."

Martha looked puzzled until the woman introduced herself. "I'm Megan O'Hara. Mr. Abbott will be home shortly. I'm to make you feel at home."

Megan O'Hara showed Martha and Charles Murdoch into a dim parlor with very stiff-looking, dark, cushioned furniture, dark wood side tables, and heavy draperies closed against the day's heat. She then brought the pair a silver tray with a porcelain teapot and delicious-looking pastries.

"I'll leave you, then," she said and left the room.

"Mr. Murdoch, where is Miss O'Hara from?"

"Ireland. She came over here a little over ten years ago because of a terrible famine. She takes care of the house for my friend Reginald, whose poor wife died in a tragic carriage accident."

"I see."

Reginald Abbott arrived an hour later. During that time, Martha walked around the parlor, looking at the small china statuettes on the fireplace mantel, the sketches on the wall, and the books in the bookcases. Everything fascinated her.

"Charles, how good to see you," boomed a cheerful voice from a round, red, sweating, smiling face. "And you must be Martha. Welcome to Brooklyn."

While the two men talked about the news of the day, Martha nodded off in a comfortable velvet plush armchair. Later, though, at dinner, she tried her best to take part in the conversation.

"Mr. Abbott," she blundered, "have you ever heard of a runaway slave by the name of Mariah who might've come through here on her way from Maryland to Canada?"

Both men froze.

"Martha," Mr. Murdoch said sternly, "there's a very important rule you must follow. Never, and I mean never, ask questions or tell stories about fugitives you might have come across. No names. No places. No nothing. It's dangerous for them, especially since the Fugitive Slave Law became so powerful."

Martha looked down in embarrassment. "I'm sorry, Mr. Murdoch."

She wondered how many more rules there were. Certainly more than she expected. And why did she, who always followed the rules, have trouble remembering them? Let's see, she counted on her fingers under the table, this made number four. Or was it numbers four, five, and six? She was beginning to lose count, and with each one she learned, she was starting to forget the others. In truth, she was beginning to hate all these rules and wanted them to stop.

Frustrated and a bit angry with these grown-ups who interrupted her every effort to obtain essential information that she needed to understand her place in the rescue, Martha excused herself to go to bed. As she left the parlor, she heard Mr. Abbott comment, "What were those Connecticut people thinking, sending a young, inexperienced girl on a rescue such as this?"

"I know," Charles Murdoch answered. "I worry,

too. She's extremely green. And although she was raised in an abolitionist home and understands the seriousness of our cause, she's not well versed in the rules and not very good at following them. She could potentially put a lot of people in danger."

"So why send her?"

"The boy to be rescued is her adopted brother. He's said to be an innocent. At age seven, he still doesn't know his letters. He gets confused easily and doesn't understand much of the world. The feeling is that she can help him to go along with the rescuers. In fact, there's some doubt we can be successful without her. Moses has so many people to protect that she'd be unable to devote all her time and energy to one small, simple boy."

"This sounds so very risky to me."

"I agree, but if anyone can handle the situation, it'll be Moses."

Once in bed, Martha tossed and turned, unable to sleep even a little bit. She stared at the ceiling, then turned onto her stomach, then tossed and turned some more. When she finally dropped off, there was Jake again. He was covered with bruises. Large and small black and blue marks covered his face, his arms, his legs. He sat alone in a dark room, huddled in a corner. She awoke with new resolve. She would conquer those "never" rules and follow them. She had to if she was going to save her brother.

Just before sunup, Martha bid farewell to Brooklyn and continued her final daylong journey with Charles Murdoch in silence. Reginald

Abbott's smaller sloop carried them around the tip of Manhattan and west to the New Jersey shore. There they hired a carriage that took them through forests and farmland until, late in the evening, they arrived in Philadelphia. Never had Martha seen such a place.

"My goodness," she screeched, "what a foul-smelling city."

"Industry, my dear," said Mr. Murdoch. "You're smelling the smoke from the factories."

"But it smells worse than just smoke, Mr. Murdoch."

"Yes, it does. These factories hire many workers, but they don't pay them very much. Other people don't even have jobs. So people are poor and they live all crowded together. And there's lots of garbage and waste."

Martha took note of the shacks too small to fit the people who lived in them. White, black, brown, no matter. She could not imagine staying even one night in such a place.

"Where will we be staying, Mr. Murdoch?"

"In a residential part of the town with folks of a higher class."

And this was so. Within fifteen minutes, the carriage pulled up before a stately three-story brick home where they were greeted by a beautifully clothed black woman. Martha struggled to hide her surprise. Except for Jake and the runaways coming through her home, she had never actually met any Afric Americans. And now that she knew the truth about herself, she was anxious to learn more about them. So she stared in a most impolite way at this woman's gingerbread-toned skin and sleek black hair tied in a bun at the nape of her neck.

In turn, the woman patted the back of her bun as if to fix it. "Is something wrong?"

"Of course not, Bertha. You look as lovely as usual," Mr. Murdoch said. "May I introduce Martha Bartlett?"

With that, Charles Murdoch pushed Martha into the home of Matthew and Bertha Smith, who immediately introduced her to Samuel and Caroline Smith, who would accompany her to Maryland. She had expected to be traveling with a white couple, and her surprise and bewilderment showed. As they all moved to the parlor for a late evening repast of lemonade and sandwiches of meat and cheese, Charles Murdoch intuited Martha's concerns.

"Martha, we've chosen to send you into Maryland with the Smiths because it's very likely that people in the South will believe you are colored. Traveling with them will help you to blend in."

"I understand," she replied although she really did not, "and the same with Mrs. Perry?"

"Yes, she's to be your aunt while you're there."

Trying to remain calm, she said, "But Mr. Murdoch, I don't know how to be a Southern colored girl."

"You aren't being someone new, Martha. You're a Northern girl visiting her aunt. That's all."

"But what if someone asks me about my skin color?"

"I don't think anyone will ask," Caroline Smith

put in, "especially since you're traveling with Samuel and myself and will be staying with Lorraine Perry. But, Martha, please, whatever you do, never, and I mean never, try to imitate the accent and manners of the local people. They'll see your error immediately. Simply be yourself."

Oh, no, thought Martha, yet another rule and still more "nevers." Did these people always have to repeat their "nevers" as if she was a child who could not understand them? Besides, by this point, it was impossible to keep track of the rules anyway. Nor was she even sure who she was anymore. White in one place, black in another?

Martha wanted nothing more than to seek out her papa's loving arms and his sage advice. A tear fell down her cheek, and her hands started to tremble. Folding them in her lap, she tried to gain enough control over herself so that she could ask to be excused to go to her room.

But that was not to be, for all of a sudden Caroline Smith asked her if she liked to read.

Swallowing hard, Martha said, "Oh, yes, ma'am. I read a great deal."

"What's your favorite book, may I ask?"

Martha did not hesitate. "*Uncle Tom's Cabin*. Mrs. Stowe told such a heartbreaking story about the slaves. I cried throughout." Therefore she was shocked to see all five pairs of adult eyes giving her a stern look.

"This was a very important test, Martha," said Caroline Smith. "Never, and I mean never, speak against slavery or let it be known that you've read about, spoken about, dreamed about, or in any other way given the issue any thought. Within a day, you'll be in Maryland. It'll be dangerous for you to let your abolitionist rearing show."

Enraged, Martha barked, "But I'm here with you, and you're abolitionists. So that was an unfair test."

"Yes, well, that may be true. But, still . . ."

"And in any case," she cut in, "what shall I say if someone asks me about slavery?"

"Simply that you're new to the area and are just learning about life there. That might open you up to a lecture about the glories of the peculiar institution, but no matter."

This was the final straw. Martha was so anxious that she needed to get away and be on her own. "I'm very perplexed," she said, "as to why you would try to trick me. It's really not right. And it's worn me out. Is it all right if I go to bed now?"

"Yes, of course," they all agreed.

Their stares of concern gave her pause, so before she left, she said, "Don't fret. I'll be fine."

Alone in her room, Martha caught a glimpse of her face in the looking glass. Walking closer to it, she sought out features that would make people think she was not white. Could it be her long black hair? Her deep brown eyes? Her cheekbones that seemed higher than her mama's or Becky's? Or was it just that her skin was not very pale? Whatever it was, Martha could finally see why some people living in a place where there were Afric people or Indians or Italians might wonder about her parentage. "Will seeing myself in a looking glass change the way I behave?" she wondered.

With these thoughts, Martha fell into a restless sleep. She dreamed of being lost in a sea of different people, but at least she had no visits from Jake. With great relief to be on her way early the next morning, she bid farewell to Mr. Murdoch and joined the Smiths for the next leg of her journey.

"Be most careful, Martha," he said as he waved goodbye.

Meanwhile, the Smiths with Martha in tow climbed into a luxurious carriage for the journey to Baltimore. As they politely explained, Afric American people were either not welcome or were treated badly on public conveyances, so they preferred to hire a private carriage if they could afford to do so. This made Martha even more curious about them, and although she was nervous about asking any more questions, she could not help herself.

"Do you live in Baltimore, Mrs. Smith?"

"Yes, dear. My husband and I own a lovely shop there. We've done quite well."

"But aren't you frightened to live there? I mean with slavery and everything."

"There are many free blacks in Baltimore, Martha. It's a big city. We're part of a warm community who support each other and those not free as well."

"How?"

"I really can't tell you any details except that we have clubs and dinners and several of us attend the same church."

Martha wanted to ask if the Smiths knew Frederick Douglass and had helped him to escape slavery, but she kept her mouth shut tight lest she be reprimanded once again. That evening, Martha and the Smiths stayed at a local farmhouse with a couple the Smiths knew. Martha suspected they were a station on the Underground Railroad, but she held her tongue, ate her meal, and then retired for the night. She dreamed once again about Jake. This time he had an iron collar around his neck attached with a chain to an iron loop in a yard. He was on his hands and knees, like a dog. Frantic that all her fears might be true, very early the next morning Martha hurried to get dressed and be on her way.

Once in Baltimore, Samuel and Caroline Smith immediately took Martha to a small sloop, giving her no time to view the city or its extremely busy port. She figured that they were as eager to see her gone as she was to reach LaGrange, get Jake, and go home. Even with a brisk westerly wind, the trip from the city to the Eastern Shore took several hours, but Martha was enchanted with the sail. Trailing her fingers in the water, she wondered if women could become sailors. After leaving the sloop, there was yet another carriage ride. Martha noted the changes as the land turned flatter and greener than up North and the air much more humid.

Finally, the long journey ended at the smallest town Martha had ever seen. Mr. Smith leaned over and whispered in her ear, "This is LaGrange. About a mile out of the town is Robert Dawes's plantation."

Martha's stomach lurched, and for the first time, she felt real fear grip her. In the early evening's dimming light, she could see that LaGrange was not at all what she had expected. It was a hodgepodge of shacks and small wood-framed shops. The streets were of dirt, as at home, but with many more ruts and loose sand blowing around in the hot breeze coming off the water. Numbers of black people were carrying bundles, the men on their backs, the women often on their turbaned heads. Most people were wearing poorly made pants, skirts, and shirts, and children were barefoot. They darted here and there, seemingly with no one watching them. Yet, if one cried or fell or got into a fight, an adult quickly came over to help them. Martha wondered how a person could tell which of these people were slaves and which free.

Martha quickly followed the Smiths to a small rundown shop with a handmade sign, "Perry's General Store." As they entered, a very thin dark woman with a scarf wrapped around her head looked up, rushed forward, put a "closed" sign on the door, and shut it firmly.

She squinted her eyes and asked in a soft voice, "Is this her?"

"This is her."

"Come, girl. I'll take you to the back to the room you'll be staying in. I need to keep the shop open for an hour or two and then we'll talk. Don't leave the room until I come for you."

"Goodbye, Martha," called Caroline Smith, all too eagerly for Martha's taste. "Enjoy your visit with your auntie Lorraine."

Martha waited in the dark musty room for Lorraine Perry to return. Although truly alone and a tad homesick, she also sensed Jake close by. He was here, just a mile away. Tomorrow, after she was rested, she would evade the adults, sneak out to LaGrange Plantation, find him, and bring him back to hide in this room. What could be so difficult if she was careful? She was 100 percent sure she could accomplish this without being seen. Then they would leave for home with Harriet Tubman.

10

THE NEXT morning, Martha sat silently, her right hand twirling one of her plaits and her foot silently tapping against the floor, while Lorraine Perry ranted. "I don't know what tomfoolery made your parents send a child your age all alone to take part in a rescue. I mean, it's not as if you've ever traveled far from home. From what I've been told, you are fresh from New England with no experience in the field."

"My parents are stationmasters on the railroad," Martha stated in her own defense. "Well, that is, until Jake came into our lives."

"I don't want to hear nothing about no railroads or anything like that. That's dangerous talk down here. Up there, too, I gather."

Martha looked down at her tightly entwined hands. "Sorry," she said. "I'm here to get Jake, and once I have him, we'll be on our way. I thought that perhaps I might go get him this morning."

Silence followed. When she looked up, she saw

Mrs. Perry's mouth hanging open in shock. After a moment, it snapped shut.

"Are you loco?" she said. "You don't just come south, walk onto a plantation, say how-de-do, and walk away with a slave. Do you know anything about how things work around here?"

"No. But Jake isn't a slave, so there shouldn't be any problem."

Even to herself, Martha sounded naive and overly optimistic, but she thought it imperative to keep up a brave and assertive front.

"Listen to me, young lady," Mrs. Perry scolded. "You are not about to go out there and put all our lives and years of hard work in jeopardy. Moses arrived in LaGrange last night. She's working on a way to retrieve Jake and then you'll go with her. The sooner, the better as far as I'm concerned. Meanwhile, you go nowhere. No. Where. Do you understand? We can't take the chance that someone will recognize you."

Martha protested, "No one knows me here."

"Well, let's see. There's Robert Dawes, of course. Oh! And there's his two side partners, Will and Tom. All three use this little town like it's their backyard. And I guess it is, come to think of it."

Mrs. Perry chuckled at her own joke, but Martha was fuming. She was perfectly aware that the further south she had traveled, the less enthusiastic her companions had become about her presence. She could not understand their hostility. After all, wasn't she here to help? Didn't Adam Burke and her own father believe that she could complete her task with the utmost success?

"Jake won't go away with just anyone. That's why I'm here."

Mrs. Perry did not agree with Martha's rationale. "We have our ways, child. We can get him away. And in any case, he's been put in the charge of his own granma, Lucy, and she's very good with the little ones. I really don't think we need you."

"Well, I'm here no matter how you might feel," she said. "Jake'll be happy to see me and he'll come with me and behave himself."

"I surely hope so. In the meantime, as I said before, stay put. I need to open my shop. Every minute it's closed means a day closer to starvation for a widow woman like myself. I'll bring you something to eat around noon."

As soon as Mrs. Perry left the living area for her shop, Martha started pacing. For an hour, she walked back and forth between the two small rooms trying to hatch a plan. It was time to act on her own instead of listening to a bunch of rules. She simply had to get out of this shop, find the plantation, and take Jake away.

In her pacing, Martha saw a small door that led to the backyard. She opened it a crack and peered out onto a storage area with an exit to the street. Putting her sunbonnet on so that it covered part of her face and checking that Jake's small carved horse and her special handkerchief were still in her pocket, she silently crept out the door and edged her way around the crates, only once bumping into a pile that threatened to tumble with a crash. She quickly pushed them back in line with her shoulder and looked around to check that Mrs. Perry had not heard anything and come to investigate. Assured that all was well, she quickly scooted out of the yard into a narrow alleyway.

There, she stopped. To her right was the way to the busy main street she had seen the day before. To her left was the way to a quiet country road. If she went that way, perhaps she would meet someone who could tell her how to get to the plantation. Almost as if planned, she ran into a young white man, nicely attired in a white suit, a white ruffled shirt, and a white top hat, which he doffed as Martha came near.

"Can I help you, sugah?" he said.

"Which way is the Dawes plantation?"

The gentleman looked puzzled. "You must be new in town. Everyone knows where that is. You sound like a Yank, in fact."

"Ah, no, suh," Martha said in what she imagined to be a Southern accent. "Ah ahhm frim dees heah pahhhhts."

The man laughed. "No, sugah, you are not from 'dees heah pahhhhts.' I can spot a Yank a mile away. What're you doin' here, anyway?"

Flustered, Martha dropped her pretense. "I'm visiting my aunt and just thought I would try to fit in. I heard the plantation here is very pretty."

"I see. Who's your aunt?"

Martha hesitated. If she said it was Lorraine Perry, this man would assume she was black. But she did not know anyone else's name.

"Auntie Lorraine is her name," she hedged.

"You mean Lorraine Perry?"

"Yes," she muttered.

Surprised, he said, "So, you're colored? Let me see." He lifted the brim of Martha's bonnet and laughed. "So you are. And lovely, indeed. Free, too. Too bad."

Martha was alarmed. "If you tell me the way, I won't take up any more of your time."

"I wouldn't mind spending time with you," he said, "but I do have business to attend to. You just walk down this road for about a mile and you'll see it. It has a long drive with Lombardy poplar trees lining each side." He doffed his hat once again and added, "Another time, perhaps?"

Martha blushed and hurried on. She had no idea what a Lombardy poplar tree was, but a long drive should certainly be easy to spot.

Being from a small town herself, Martha should have remembered that news travels fast—that tongues wag as happily as the tail of a friendly dog. But she had only one thought in mind, and that was to find Jake. So she hurried down the road, getting no further than a quarter of a mile when she heard those horses' hooves she dreaded so much and saw two frighteningly familiar faces looming above her—Will and Tom, the slave catchers.

"Well, well, well. Miss Martha Bartlett. Lookin' for someone?" said Will with a huge leering smile.

Martha gulped. "I think you have me confused with someone else."

"Somehow I don't think so. We've been expecting someone from your part of the world, but never in a million years did I think it would be you. Are you alone?"

Martha ignored the question and turned back in the direction she had come, practically running down the road. But she was no match for the two large men on horseback. Will quickly caught up with her and scooped her up onto his horse, holding her tightly around her waist. Martha could smell the dirt and sweat of his body, and his breath did not please her either.

"You'd better come with us," he said. "I'm sure Mr. Dawes will be pleased to see you." And he laughed that laugh she had heard way back in Liberty Falls the morning after Jake was born.

Within minutes, Martha saw the drive with the poplar trees, so tall and pretty and shady. A few gallops more, and the LaGrange Plantation house came into view. It was bigger than any house she had ever seen, even the brownstone in Brooklyn, New York. Broad and white with a huge wraparound veranda, it soared up two high stories. Four columns held up the overhanging roof, and rows and rows of paned glass windows lined each floor, the ones on the ground level twice as high as the ones above.

As Will and Tom dragged her up to the front door, a group of slave children gathered to gawk. They were no older than five, she thought, and all wore drab shabby sack-like dresses that looked to be made of either wool or cotton, Martha was not sure which. None had shoes. She thought about Jake, wondering if he looked wide-eyed and hungry like these youngsters.

A better-dressed man opened the door and gazed expressionless at Martha.

"Massa Dawes saw you ride up. He says you should come into the parlor."

To Martha, the parlor looked more like a room in the palaces she read about in her schoolbooks. The ceiling was very high and candelabras hung down in several places. The furniture was plush and ornate.

As she gaped, her mouth open wide enough to catch more than a few flies, she heard another familiar voice.

"What did you two boys bring me?"

Martha spun around to see Robert Dawes slumped leisurely in a comfortable club chair, his legs stretching out forever. In his left hand, he held a newspaper. In his right was a drink in a tall crystal glass. Martha wished he would offer her something to wet her parched throat.

"A little gift from Connecticut, Mr. Dawes. Found her lurking around on the back road from town. Seems strange that she appears to be here by herself."

"Thanks, boys. You did fine by bringing her here. Wait outside, and close the door behind you."

The two men left, but not before each walked right up to Martha and gave her a big-toothed grin. Then she heard Dawes's soft, withering voice.

"I remember you. You're Jake's self-proclaimed sister."

Martha's throat clutched as he slowly rose to his feet, towering over her. His brown jodhpurs, white blousy long-sleeved shirt, blue satin brocaded vest, and knee-high leather boots matched the wealth of his home.

"I'm not *self-proclaimed*," she heard herself answer. "I *am* his sister. Have been his entire life."

"I think not," he responded. "That little boy is *my* son and my *slave*, and he belongs to me. But haven't we been through this before?"

Dawes was a man like none other Martha had encountered. She hated his arrogance and disdain for other people. As he walked to the window and looked out over his lush green lawn, he added, "I'd ask what you're doing here and who else came with you, but those'd probably be stupid questions."

"I've come to get Jake."

"I think not," he repeated.

"What do you want him for? He's probably being troublesome."

"Not so much now, but certainly on our way here. Almost wore me out."

Martha had to laugh. "So let me remove him from you, then."

"No."

She got serious again. "Why not?"

"I could answer that I generally don't give away slaves. After all, what would people think if I did that? Every slave I own would be assuming I'd give them their freedom. But I'm also hoping that with him here, Mariah'll come back to look for him."

Martha could not believe what she'd heard. "She can't do that. The woman who birthed Jake is dead. And none of us knows for sure if she was this Mariah you keep talking about."

His body tensed. "She's dead?"

"The woman who had Jake died in childbirth. She's buried back in the town cemetery."

"I was thinking maybe you folks were hiding her somewhere or maybe she had gone up to Canada."

"Why would she have left her baby behind? And anyway, maybe your Mariah wasn't Jake's mother."

"Yes, she was. He looks just like her. Even her own mama can see that."

"This is all beside the point," Martha changed the topic and spoke in a more childlike manner. "Now that you know she's gone, can I please have Jake? Then I'll leave."

"No. He may be of value to me someday. To sell. To use here. I don't know."

"Jake can't do much. Surely, you've noticed that he's slow and doesn't learn things well, if at all. Anyway, we offered to purchase him. Isn't our money good enough for you?"

Martha caught Dawes's confused and saddened look before he turned away. For some moments, he ignored her, taking time to pick up his now empty glass, fill it again from a decanter on a nearby table, gulp the liquid down, and refill it again. Martha felt a chill as he strode so close to her that she could smell something strong and unfamiliar on his breath and see how his eyes had become unfocused. Was what he was drinking spirits? Her mama and papa had warned her about the evils of alcohol. It was not permitted anywhere in Liberty Falls.

"How old are you, Martha? Thirteen, fourteen?"

"I'll be fourteen next month," she responded.

"Ah," he said. "That was Mariah's age when I first

realized how attractive she was. Every time she was near me, I wanted to reach out and touch her, but she acted as if I repelled her. The more she shrank away, the more I wanted her."

As he moved closer, Martha took a step back. Every nerve in her body buzzed with fear. Should she run for the door? Were Will and Tom guarding it? Hoping he would not notice, she began to slowly inch her way across the room, making her steps as tiny as she could.

"You know," he said softly, "I loved Mariah. She was so beautiful, not just in her body, but her spirit, too. She had a glow about her."

Martha had never heard such intimate sentiments come out of the mouth of any man. She was shocked and frightened and had no idea how to respond to him. Then she remembered Adam Burke saying that slave owners had a different way of thinking than other people and that to communicate with them, a person had to speak their language and play their game. Frantically seeking the right words, she sputtered out, "Well, if you loved her so, why didn't you free her? Then you could've courted her and maybe she would've come to reciprocate your feelings."

Dawes leaned his head back and laughed. "You're sure one innocent girl. First, I couldn't marry a colored girl, a slave no less. Second, I was already married with three boys of my own. Third," and here Martha heard him take in a long breath, "if I freed her, she would have left me. She hated me."

She almost felt sorry for this man who so obviously had passionate feelings for Jake's mother.

Almost, but not quite. She screwed up her courage and tried to imitate the cool, sophisticated manner in which Caroline Smith spoke. Maybe that would make him move away from her.

"Surely not, Mr. Dawes. You're a most attractive man, and you have lots of money. Maybe if you'd been nice to her, she wouldn't have hated you."

Dawes took another long drink from his glass while Martha's own throat burned with thirst. At last he said, "It's of no matter now. I wanted her, and so I set out to take her. When she refused me, I threatened to whip or even sell her mother. So she complied. When she became with child, my wife, who knew what I was up to, demanded I sell her. That's why Mariah ran away."

"Maybe she ran away so that her child—and *your* child—wouldn't be a slave."

Martha jumped as Dawes angrily shouted, "Why am I telling you these things? What kind of Northern witch are you?"

She looked down and continued her minute steps toward the door. Dawes stared at her for some moments in deep thought. "You know. You remind me a bit of Mariah." Martha shuddered as he once again gained ground on her. "You're not thin like her, but you are young and innocent and you do have intriguing curves."

Martha froze as he placed his face next to hers, his breath hot on her cheek. He traced his long thin finger down her face and cheeks, and then further down her neck. She leapt away, her heart thumping so hard she thought it would burst through her skin.

Dawes laughed again. "Ah, little Martha. What am I going to do with you now?"

Martha's voice shook. "Let me go back to the town with Jake. After all, you don't want your wife to see me, do you?"

"She's not here. Takes the children up to the Virginia mountains in this heat."

"Has she seen Jake?"

"Not yet. I know she won't be happy when she does. She'll probably insist I sell him right away. She hated Mariah. In fact, she hates all the young slave girls. If she had her way, I would sell them as soon as they reached ten."

Again, he laughed. Martha was appalled. Dawes's scary behavior added urgency to her quest. She needed to get Jake and herself away from him as quickly as possible.

Dawes, meanwhile, continued with his drinking. Martha saw him stumble before saying, "Until I can figure out what to do with you, I need to keep you someplace where you won't cause any more trouble."

He opened the parlor door and called in Will and Tom. "Take her to the woodshed out back and bar the door so she can't get out."

Will looked gleeful. "Chain her up?" he asked.

"That's not necessary. And don't you boys rough her up or anything. I just need time to think."

"Mr. Dawes," Martha pleaded frantically, "don't do this. The law will be coming to look for me real soon. You'll be in deep trouble."

"You don't understand, Martha. In LaGrange, I *am* the law."

Within minutes, Martha found herself tossed into a small, dark, musty storehouse with just one tiny window near the ceiling way above her head. There were no lamps, no furniture, nothing but a few sawed-up logs and some old sawdust scattered around the floor. She rushed to the door and pushed, pulled, and pounded on it but it was all to no avail. She shouted until she was hoarse and then broke down in tears. What was there for her now?

For the rest of the day and into the night, Martha huddled on the floor, away from the ants crawling over the logs. She was hungry, thirsty, hot, then cold, and terrified, especially by the footsteps that crossed the door's path several times, paused, and then continued on. She welcomed the light from the full moon that eventually made its way across the sky and shone in the small window. At least then she could make out her own fingers as they nervously twisted through her hair, loosening her plaits. What a mess she had created! Now she was the one who needed rescuing.

Finally, sometime late into the night, she heard the bar being quietly removed from the door. As it opened, she saw the outline of a tall, thin woman come limping in. When the fading moonlight lit her face, Martha gave out a scream and then quickly covered her mouth with her hands. The woman standing before her looked exactly like the runaway slave who had come to her house the night that Jake was born. She would never in a million years forget that face.

"Chile, you look like you seen a ghost," said a soft voice.

"Who are you?"

"Can't you tell? I'm Lucy, Jake's granma. But you thought I was Mariah, didn't you?"

Martha's heart beat quickly and her breath came in short gasps. "Yes," she replied. In the dim light, she could see her mistake. This woman was much older than the girl she remembered.

Lucy stepped closer and gave Martha a hard look. "I didn't expect to see a colored girl. Jake keeps talkin' about his family being white."

"Yes. Well. It's a long story."

"We don' have time for no long stories."

At that moment, Martha caught the whiff of smoke and ashes. "What's that smell?"

"A fire in town. Started at Lorraine Perry's and spreading like wild fire."

Martha was horrified.

"You know, don't you," Lucy said. "Massa Dawes wanted to send a message to us all."

"Is Mrs. Perry all right?"

"I dunno. Won't know 'til morning. But she has no home now and no livelihood, that's for sure."

Martha was so ashamed she could not look Lucy in the face.

"We don't have but a little bit of time," Lucy said. "Here, drink this water. Fast."

As Martha gulped down the liquid and ate a piece of cornbread, the older woman said, "I have to get you outta here. But first I need to know about my Mariah. I heard tell you told Massa Dawes she's dead."

"Yes."

"Tell me about her."

"I was just a little girl, Miss Lucy. Just six. She came to our house to hide on her way further North. My parents and aunt and uncle took her up to the attic. She was in great pain. I was peeking from my bedroom and she looked at me. Just one look. She tried to smile, but then another pain came."

Lucy's eyes filled with tears. "Then what?"

"I heard lots of moans and then after a long time a scream. Then nothing until finally I heard a baby cry."

By now the tears were streaming freely down Lucy's cheeks. "She was such a beautiful chile. About your age when that monster started pushing hisself on her. Just fifteen or so when she became with chile. Just a chile herself."

Martha remained silent while Lucy took time to wipe her eyes.

"I 'member he even gave her a beautiful red silk embroidered shawl. I tole her to give it back, but she wouldn't. She'd never had anything so precious before."

Martha gave a loud gasp.

"What's the matter?" Lucy asked.

"I saw that shawl the night she came to our house. Oh, Miss Lucy, I'm so sorry." She quickly added, "My papa and uncle buried her and said prayers for her."

"That's good," Lucy responded.

After a moment, she knelt by Martha and took her hands. "We'll have only a short time to get you and Jake outta here. So we gotta hurry."

"Where is he, Miss Lucy? How is he?"

"He's fine. When he first got here, he was silent and angry. But Massa Dawes let me take care of him, said to teach him about the kitchen. He been better since then. He's a good boy."

"Really?"

Lucy gave a small smile. "A real good helper. And smart."

"Smart?"

"I been teaching him about herbs and such. He takes to it good."

Martha was so surprised she could think of nothing to say.

"Anyway, we need to go *now*. Jake is waiting for us in the woods behind the house. Hurry up."

"Where am I going? Will we meet Moses?"

"Moses done left hours ago. She had five others waiting to run and no one could find you. Come on."

A confused Martha followed Lucy to the back of the house, and there was Jake. He was wearing the clothes that he had on the day he was kidnapped. They were a bit ragged but clean and now too short for him. He was barefoot, his shoes somehow gone missing. Other than being somewhat taller, he looked the same. Not underfed, as she had expected. Not black and blue. For sure, Lucy had protected and cared for him as best she could.

When he saw Martha, Jake ran to her, wrapping his arms around her waist.

"Mattie. Mattie," he sobbed. "Why did you let him take me?"

"I'm so sorry, Jake," she sobbed in turn. "But I've

come for you now. To take you home. We can talk about everything later, but now we have to be quick and leave."

"But I don't wanna leave my granma. Can she come with us?"

Martha looked at Lucy. She liked the idea of having this person who knew the way out come along with her. "Yes, will you come, Miss Lucy?"

Lucy knelt down next to Jake and took him into her arms.

"Chile, I can't go with you. Not with my bad leg. And I'm too old to make the journey."

"Maybe I can help you walk, Miss Lucy," Martha offered.

"No. Leg's all mangled. I tried to run away from Massa Dawes's father. Got caught. He ordered his men to break it with a sledgehammer so's I couldn't run away again but so's I could walk good enough to cook for him."

"I'm so sorry."

Lucy stood and said pointedly, "Not your fault, though other things are. Now, you all gotta get going. Here's a little sack with some bread and a rope and knife that you might need. No meat to attract animals."

Martha shuddered as she took the burlap bag. "Where will we go?"

"North."

Martha was silent, sorry for her lack of patience and her always impetuous actions.

"How'll we go north? Who'll take us?"

"You," Lucy answered. "You'll follow the drinking gourd and the North Star and take Jake north on the Underground Railroad. My sweet Mariah fought for that, and so will you. Some miles north you'll see a small red farmhouse. Go there. Miz Holden'll help you."

"But how do I get there?"

"You go through these here woods, keeping the fields on your right 'til they end. Then you keep going straight, cross the river, and keep going 'til you come to a road. You'll see the farmhouse. If Miz Holden has a blue quilt on the line, it's safe to come on. If not, hide in the woods 'til she puts it up."

"What if we get lost?"

"Just follow the North Star. And only travel by night. If you get lost or delayed, you stay put during the day."

"Won't they come after us?"

"Sure thing. But with the fire burning, everyone'll be busy 'til daybreak. They might not miss you for a whole day. When they do find you gone, Will and Tom'll come after you with the dogs. So try to walk in the river as soon as you can so's the dogs lose your scent."

Martha had never felt so frightened in her life.

"You gotta go now, girl."

"But what'll happen to you, Miss Lucy?"

"It don' matter. Massa can whup me, sell me, or do anythin' he likes. All that's important is that Jake goes north. Besides," she said as an afterthought, "Massa sure likes my cookin', so he probly won' sell me."

Lucy drew Jake into her arms one last time. "You jes remember, chile. I loves you and always will."

With that, Lucy rose and pushed Martha toward the woods. "I'll pray for you," she said and turned back to the big house. Martha took Jake's hand and said, "Come on, Jake. Let's go."

Only then did she realize that in the fire she, too, had lost all she had, but most importantly, the papers saying she and Jake were free.

CHAPTER

MARTHA SHIFTED her weight from one foot to another as she peered into those dark, frightening woods. She hated woods. Always had. When she was a small child, her papa had a hard time getting her to take strolls with him in the Connecticut forests. He had to coax her with promises of finding pretty flowers and having sweet snacks when they returned home. Still, to this very moment, she cringed when she thought about the feel of the plants and trees brushing against her skin and all the insects, animals, and reptiles waiting to pounce on her.

Jake tugged at her sleeve. "Let's go, Mattie. You said we should hurry."

Martha stared at him and the forest and froze. Jake ran into the woods. "C'mon, Mattie," he called.

Her voice cracking with fright, she yelled after him, "Jake, wait for me. Stop! Come back here."

When Jake scurried back to her side, she grabbed him by the arm, placed her hands on his shoulders, and spoke firmly into his face. That was the only way she could be certain he was paying attention.

"Calm down. We can't just go running off into the woods. We have to stay close together and think things through first."

Martha opened the sack Lucy had given her and took out the rope. "Now, I'm gonna tie this around your waist and . . ."

"No," shouted Jake. "I don't want a rope. I don't like them."

Martha grabbed him in panic, but Jake pulled away from her. He started shaking his hands up and down and rocking back and forth on the balls and heels of his bare feet. Martha had to stop him before his habitual moans, then shrieks, followed. "Jake," she urged, "I want to tie the other end to me, so that we won't get separated."

Jake just moaned and whined and rocked. Suddenly, there came a loud rustling in the undergrowth. Frantically, Martha jerked Jake toward a tree they could hide behind, her hand quickly covering his mouth to quell his noise.

"What're you chirren doing?" came Lucy's angry voice. In no time at all, she stood before the crouching Martha and Jake and pulled them to their feet. "I told you to get goin' and here you are yellin' and screamin' so loud that someone's bound to hear you."

Jake ran to Lucy and threw his arms around her hips. "She wants to tie me with a rope. I don't want no rope, Granma. I don't wanna go with her. Can't I stay with you?"

Martha was livid. It was like old times when she

got blamed for Jake's doings. She was very tempted to agree with him. Why not let Lucy take him? Maybe he'd be better off with her.

"Hush, chile," Lucy said. "Everything'll be all right. You know you need to leave this place and go back up North. That's what your mama Mariah wanted for you."

Jake just held on tighter, tears now coursing down his cheeks. Humiliated, Martha waited for the reprimand she knew was coming.

"And as for you, Missy Martha, you get yourself together and take this boy home." She then untied the rope from Jake's waist and threw it at her. "And don' you treat my boy here like no slave. He free and he gonna stay free."

Martha looked down at the ground. "I'm sorry, Miss Lucy, but it's dark and I don't know where I'm going. I'm scared of losing Jake and getting lost myself."

"You gotta trust the boy. And he gotta trust you. I taught Jake something about these woods. He can help you. Now, get going."

Martha reluctantly headed into the dense woods. As she put her first foot forward, she realized that this was the moment she had been waiting for. So many times on this journey she had wanted the adults to leave her be so she could make her own decisions. Now, they had. She gathered her courage and looked at Jake. He was still crying, and it was all her fault. She had to be strong, but patient, with him. No more hands on hips. No more thumping foot. Just a firm gentleness, she thought. The important thing was to lead him home. Starting now. Slowly, she took her treasured handkerchief from her pocket and gently wiped his eyes. She squeezed his fingers as she had so many times in the past, and although she felt his shoulders tense, he allowed her to hold on to him.

Before she disappeared into the darkness, Martha looked back. There was Lucy wringing her hands and watching until she was sure they were on their way. In the stillness, Martha heard her say softly, as if in prayer, "And please, you chirren, go quietly and be careful and be safe."

After about a half hour of blindly following a narrow path, Martha stopped short. It was time to see if Jake had really learned anything from Lucy.

"Jake, I'm not sure where we are. Do you think we're going north? These trees are so big, I can't really see the sky or the North Star."

"Granma Lucy taught me a trick about the trees. Wanna hear it?"

"Tell me."

"See, Mattie. See the moss on this tree?"

"Uh-huh."

"Well, the moss points north. See, there's not so much moss on the other side of the tree. Sometimes none at all."

Martha still did not trust Jake's abilities. "Let me see."

Much to her surprise, she saw that on one side of all the trees around her, there was thick green moss.

"So, what you're saying is that we walk in that direction? The way the moss is pointing."

"That's what Granma said. She said it might be useful to me someday."

"Your granma's very smart, Jake. Let's go."

Onward they went deeper into the woods, stepping as quietly as they could. Still, the twigs under their feet snapped and cracked and small rocks and pebbles made scrunching noises as they passed over them. Martha constantly fanned gnats and mosquitoes away from her face and arms while Jake noisily slapped at them. Every few minutes Martha shushed Jake and he shushed her right back in a louder voice. Martha paused at practically every tree to check for moss and at every other tree to look up through the overhanging branches hoping to glimpse a piece of the sky and maybe the North Star. A gathering fog from the marshy swamps on either side of their path did not help. Martha wheezed and gasped as the thick humid air clogged her lungs. Often, the two had to stop for her to catch her breath. Jake followed along, not once complaining about her slowness.

During one stop, Martha heard a faraway braying and howling that alerted her to danger. "What's that?"

"Mattie, it sounds like Mr. Dawes's dogs. I heard them every time he brought them into the yard."

Martha thought of the fugitive slave stories she had read, of the bloodhounds tracking the runaways. A shot of fear almost paralyzed her. Lucy had predicted that the fire would prevent Dawes from discovering their absence until the next morning, but she was wrong.

Jake looked up at her in fright. "Those are scary dogs. They're big and they sniff all around you."

"How do you know that?"

"I was outside once when they came by. They sniffed me and stuck their noses in my face. They growled at me."

Martha froze. These dogs would most likely recognize Jake's scent. She thought quickly.

"We need to find someplace to hide," she said.

"Remember, Mattie, Granma Lucy said we should walk in the river so the dogs won't be able to smell us."

"But where's the river?"

Jake tugged on her arm, dragging her forward. He looked terrified.

"One time Granma Lucy took me in the woods," he said, "and she told me that if I followed where the moss told me to go, I would get to a river. She said that it wasn't too deep in most places."

"Thank you, Miss Lucy," Martha thought to herself. "Thank you for preparing Jake for this very day."

The sound of the hounds grew closer. Martha moved faster than she thought was possible, sometimes leading, other times following Jake. At the point at which she thought she would collapse from the effort, Jake stopped dead.

"Why are you stopping? If we stop, I won't be able to get myself moving again."

Pointing his finger, he said, "Listen, Mattie. The river."

Together, they broke through a group of dense trees and there it was, a fast-moving river about as wide as their barn back home. Although there were numerous rocks poking up on both shores, Martha did not see any in the middle, so she could not fathom a guess as to how deep it was.

Martha's experience with rivers was not great. In truth, they scared her as so many things did. She had dipped her feet into Blackwell's Brook with Caleb, but she had never gone swimming and never thought she would. That would require removing some of her clothing, and Martha, like all the girls she knew, simply would never entertain such an improper thought. But she needed to cross that river, not just to save Jake, but to save herself.

Gritting her teeth, she put one foot then the other into the water. It was cold like mountain water, and the current felt strong. She paused, then looked at Jake rocking from one foot to the other and shaking his hands up and down. She drew him to her and hugged him firmly. "I know you'll hate this, Jake, but we must tie the rope around each of our waists so that neither one of us gets carried away by the river and drowns. Will you let me do that?"

Martha heard the dogs more clearly now. So did Jake.

"Put it around your waist first," he moaned.

After several tries with her nervous fingers, she had it tied tightly around her waist. She then quickly secured her sack and turned to Jake. "Ready?"

"I guess." While she tied the rope, he continued his moaning almost in a whisper and then quieted down.

Turning her back to him, she said, "Now, put your arms around my neck and wrap your legs around my waist."

Jake did as he was told, and once he was secured onto her back, Martha strode into the river. He was so light that at first the crossing was easy. The rocks were relatively flat and she moved forward without any problems. But as she got further in and the water rose, her shoes acted like iron weights, slowing her down. Using all the determination she could muster, she continued north on the crossing, the water rising higher and higher. Jake began to whimper, and his arms and legs tightened around her.

"Don't hold on so tight, Jake. You're choking me," she said. "And try to lift your body up. That way, maybe I can move a little faster."

A tree branch rushed by, catching Martha's arm. She pushed it away but it left a bright red streak of blood running down to her hand. She swiped at it, missed a step, and, twisting her ankle, lost her balance. The river grabbed her and pushed her downstream. She thought she would drown as water rushed into her mouth and up her nose. A long, thick tree trunk that had fallen into the river loomed up in front of her. She threw her arms around it. Its bare branches scratched her face and a thick limb hit Jake on the head. He slumped against her and Martha's throat seized up with terror.

"Jake, are you all right?"

Jake was silent. Martha struggled to reestablish her footing. The water was up to her neck and she was using her arms to boost Jake's body and head above the water line, praying he was still alive. Once steady, she waded forward for what seemed like hours but the dogs' barks lessened and she hoped that meant they had lost the scent.

At long last, the water lowered and the land rose, the bottom of the riverbed becoming softer, but muddier. Exhausted, Martha reached the north shore, using every last bit of her strength to drag herself and Jake out of the water and up to a sandy spot behind a large rock. There she loosened her grip on him and gently lowered him to the ground. She attempted to undo the rope, but the water had tightened the knots and so Martha reached for the knife in her small sack, carefully unwrapped it from its cloth covering, and used its sharp blade to cut through the strong twine. Perhaps, she thought, it was not wise to cut the rope, but for both their sakes, she had to. If Jake woke up still tethered to her, he was bound to panic and cry out.

Making sure that Jake was still breathing, Martha lay down beside him to give him warmth from her body. She rubbed his arms and legs and spoke loudly into his ear. He did not move. Worn out and despondent, Martha determined to keep watch, but instead she quickly fell into a deep, dreamless sleep. When she woke up to bright sunlight, Jake was staring at her.

"I'm hungry," he said.

Martha started laughing.

"Shhhhhh."

She lowered her voice. "Jake, how's your head?"

"I'm fine, Mattie. Did something happen to me?"

"A tree limb hit your head and knocked you out. I was real worried about you."

Jake ran his fingers over his head. "I feel a lump here," he pointed, "but it doesn't hurt. And anyway, I'm hungry."

Martha opened the sack, although she already knew that the bread Lucy had given her would be totally disintegrated, and it was. "I'm afraid we don't have anything. Just water from the river, but I'm not sure we should expose ourselves to whoever might be watching."

Jake looked around and crooked his neck to listen. "It's real quiet, Mattie. I think it would be safe for me to go drink some water. I'm really, really thirsty."

Martha was not so sure, but they could not go for a whole day without at least some water. "All right, but I'll go with you."

Without thinking, she started to get up. A pain shot through her ankle and up her leg. Jake bent down to take a look. "What happened?"

"I sprained my ankle on a rock in the river. What'll we do now?"

"I'll be right back."

Martha chewed her lip and started to protest.

Jake stiffened his back and said, "Remember, Mattie, Granma Lucy said you have to trust me."

He then scampered off and when he came back, he had two sturdy tree branches that forked at the tops. "Try this. Maybe it'll help you walk."

Sure enough. Even though one tree limb was taller and thicker than the other, Martha could use them as crutches, but they sure would be moving very slowly.

"I found something else," Jake said. "Some mushrooms."

"But aren't they supposed to be poisonous?"

"Granma Lucy showed me some different ones. These are safe. I already ate some, and see? I'm not dead or even sick." Then he held out a cloth dripping with water. "And I soaked this handkerchief in the river so we can suck on it for water."

"Granma Lucy again?"

"She taught me lots of things, Mattie, about the trees and plants and even about some animals. I found some berries that I can pick later and we can have those to eat, too."

"That sounds good, Jake. You're really smart."

Beaming with pride, Jake asked, "When do we leave here, Mattie?"

"Tonight. We'll just have to stay put behind this rock and hope that no one comes looking for us."

"There's a bigger rock a little bit further into the woods. Maybe we should hide there."

Martha hesitated as she gazed into the leafy darkness. "I guess that's a good idea," she said, "but first, let's try to dry some of our clothes in the sun and then we'll move."

For the rest of the morning, Martha and Jake turned this way and that in the small spot of sunlight behind the rock until their clothes dried. By noon, with Jake's help, Martha had hobbled to the larger boulder, and there they spent the rest of the day sleeping on and off and talking in low voices.

"Jake, can you tell me," she asked gently, "how Dawes treated you after he took you away from us?"

Jake shrugged. "I don't remember."

Martha persisted. "You must remember something."

"He wasn't so nice to me, Mattie, and that Will man was even worse. I don't wanna remember it."

The two sat in thought for a while. Then Jake broke the silence.

"He hit me, Mattie."

"Dawes hit you?"

"No, not him. The Will man. It was right after they took me in the carriage. I tried to get away, and the Will man hit me."

"Dawes told him to do that?"

"No. Mr. Dawes, he made him stop."

At that moment, Martha hated Will even more than she had before. But Dawes? He surprised her.

Jake pulled his bent legs up to his chest and wrapped his arms around them. Then he began a soft, slow swaying. "Then on the boat? I tried to push that Will man away and I guess I vexed him something awful 'cause he locked me in the cabin for a long time. It got real dark, and I was so scared and I screamed and yelled. Mr. Dawes, he found me and told that Will man to leave me alone."

Again, Martha was surprised that Dawes had shown Jake some compassion, but she was furious at Will. Someday, she promised herself, she would get even with him, even if it was the last thing she ever did.

Martha gently stroked Jake's arms and legs. "I'm so sorry, Jake. I shouldn't have left you alone to use the privy. Not for even a second. All of this is my fault."

"It isn't *your* fault, Mattie. That Will man is just wicked."

Martha turned her face away so Jake would not see her tears.

"Anyway, Mr. Dawes wasn't so bad. When I got to the big house, Granma Lucy was there. And when she saw me, she cried and asked him if she could take care of me."

"And he agreed?"

"Uh-huh. He said I was of no use. That I couldn't understand anything, but maybe she could use me in the kitchen. Told her to keep me outta his sight. I was glad." He paused for a moment. "Mattie, why do people always say mean things about me? Calling me simple and saying I can't learn things."

Martha hesitated. How could she tell Jake he was somehow damaged in his brain? "It means you're a special boy, Jake, one that some people can't appreciate."

She knew she had not given a suitable answer, but Jake smiled as if she had praised him.

Martha redirected the conversation. "Why do you call Lucy 'granma'?"

"I dunno. I don't really know what a granma is. We never had none, right?"

"That's so."

"Anyway, she told me I was her daughter Mariah's child and that made me her grandson. I told her she was wrong and that my mama's name is Sarah."

Martha nodded.

"Well, then she took me to a looking glass. It was really interesting, Mattie. We don't have one, do we?"

"No. Mama says it would make us self-loving to always be looking at ourselves. But Becky showed me hers once. It was wonderful."

"It sure is. Granma showed me how she and me look a little the same. And she said that because of that, I could call her granma. So I did."

"Did you live with her?"

"Uh-huh. Down with the slaves. Like her. They were all nice to me. I slept on the floor and I lost my shoes and I had no toys. But when I felt sad, she took me on her lap and sang to me and hugged me and I felt better."

"I'm so glad you had her, Jake. And she was fortunate to have you, too."

"I s'pose. But I missed you, Mattie. And Mama. And Papa. And Caleb."

He should know the truth about himself, Martha

thought, and he would. As soon as they got home, she would insist that their papa and mama explain it all to him. Maybe that would help her mama get well again, too. For now, though, Martha took hold of his hand and squeezed it. "I missed you, too. We all did. We've been looking for you for months."

"And that's why you came to get me? 'Cause you missed me?"

Martha nodded and took him into her arms.

"And I don't wanna remember those wicked men anymore. Is that all right, Mattie?"

"Yes, Jake. No more remembering."

For a few long minutes, they were silent. Then Martha heard a sniffling and felt Jake's body quiver as he cried for a good long while. When he stopped, he said, "Mattie, I don't like slavery."

"I know, Jake. None of us do."

"But I never really knew what it was until now. It was just something Mama and Papa talked about. That it was bad. But I didn't understand. I don't wanna be a slave, Mattie. Please don't let them make me a slave."

"Don't fret so, Jake. We're going home, and no one will make you a slave. I promise."

It took some time for Jake to stop shaking, and for Martha to realize that this was the first time they had ever had a serious conversation. It was a revelation. Yes, he was still not like other children. He could not read and was easily confused by what she said. And yet he had conveyed deep feelings, a great deal of fear, and an unexpected eagerness to forgive and forget. Lucy had recognized Jake's special qualities. Martha had a lot to learn from her example.

Late in the afternoon, Martha awoke with a start from another fitful nap. She was so afraid of losing Jake again that she could hardly close her eyes. Looking around anxiously, she spotted him busy playing with something on top of a nearby low stone.

"What are you doing, Jake?" she asked.

"I made us some dinner, Mattie."

Martha sat up, her foot hurting something fierce. She tried to remove her shoe, but it would not budge. Panic gripped her. How would she ever be able to walk?

"What's the matter?"

"My foot's real bad. I hope I'll be able to make it out of these woods."

He looked at her with his big eyes. "You will, Mattie. I'll help you."

"I know you will." Martha paused. "So," she winced, "what did you make us?" She was imagining a play meal of rocks and leaves, but instead she saw a nicely laid out meal of things she did not recognize.

"Well, here're some greens I picked by the water's edge. Taste real good, like mint. And here're some huckleberries I found on the ground, and some nuts."

"This looks really good, Jake," she smiled.

"Granma Lucy was even teaching me to cook, Mattie."

"Cook?"

"Uh-huh. And I like it. Maybe I can cook something for you someday."

"I would like that very much, Jake."

As Jake sat cross-legged on the ground, Martha gasped. The bottoms of his feet were all cut up. She felt ashamed that she had given no thought to his being without shoes. Blood was slowly oozing from several of the wounds. Even as a child, Jake reacted to pain differently than other children. He might moan when he saw some visible sign of injury, but when he did not, he simply ignored it.

"What happened to your feet?"

Martha saw Jake's puzzled look as he turned the bottoms up and stared at them. "I dunno. Must've cut them on those burrs over there near the sweetgum trees."

"Sweetgum trees?"

"Uh-huh. Those over there."

Martha looked at the green tree with its hard, spiked fallen fruits surrounding its trunk. There were dozens of them, and Jake had walked among them without a thought to any discomfort he might have experienced. Martha reached for her underskirt and with great effort tore off a large swath of it.

"Mattie, what're you doing to your clothes?"

"I'm gonna make you some shoes."

She tore the length of muslin into two long strips and gently wrapped one around each of Jake's feet. They would at least cushion him from the rocks and sharp burrs.

"Try 'em out."

Martha watched as Jake hopped around on one foot, then the other.

"They're very comfortable, Mattie. Thanks."

Next, Martha and Jake ate the meal he had prepared and sucked water from the cloth he dunked in the river time and time again. As soon as it got dark, they once again headed off through the forest. At a semi-clearing near some marshlands, the tall oaks and pines lessened so that Martha could see the sky.

"Jake, there it is. See it? The North Star. We're heading in the right direction."

Four hours of painful struggle later, Martha's ankle was so swollen that she could hardly put her foot on the ground. The two crutches that Jake had found for her were a godsend, but they would not hold up much longer. With each step she took, she could feel them bend and hear them crack under her weight. Finally, she touched Jake gently on the shoulder.

"I need to rest, Jake. Just for a bit and then we'll move on."

The two collapsed behind another huge rock. For some minutes, they listened to the cicadas and crickets, whose loud, eerie songs Martha knew from back home. There were any number of other insect noises she did not know and which gave her the shivers. From time to time, a noise jolted her to attention, but all she saw were a few rabbits hopping by and a beautiful doe with two fawn. Although Martha had not lost her fear of the woods, now she was oddly comforted by them. The thicker the growth, the safer she felt from the slave catchers and their dogs.

"Jake," she said as they rested, "wanna hear a few conundrums?"

"Oh, yes, Mattie. Maybe I'll guess the answers."

Martha knew that Jake could never figure out the answers to these riddles, but he always loved to try.

"Okay. Here we go. Why is a cook like a barber?"

Jake thought and thought and then his face lit up. "I dunno. Tell me."

Martha had expected this exact reply. This was always how they played the game.

"Because he dresses hare. Get it? *Hare* like in another name for rabbit."

Jake laughed and then shushed himself. "I get it. Tell me another one."

"Okay. What is the difference between a stubborn horse and a postage stamp?"

"Ummmmmm. I dunno. Tell me."

"You lick one with a stick, and stick the other with a lick."

Jake laughed so much he had to cover his mouth to muffle the sound. Finally, he giggled, "Tell me another one."

"One more and then we have to head off. Why may a slap on the side of the head be considered equivalent in worth to gold?"

Jake grinned at her again, jumping up and down on his crossed legs like a little spring toy. "Tell me."

"Because it makes the ear ring."

Martha wondered how Jake could laugh at these conundrums he did not understand. It was the spirit of them, she guessed. He liked feeling part of something, the give and take that did not include being told to be quiet, to sit down, to behave.

"Time to go," Martha said as she struggled to her feet and placed her makeshift crutches under her armpits.

On they went until, close to daybreak, they reached a small open field that ended in a dirt road. Three cows stood under a tree moving only to lower their heads to munch some grass. Across the road was a small red clapboard farmhouse with a yellow quilt hanging on a line strung across two trees.

"Look, Jake. I think that's the house Lucy told us to look for. But I don't think that the quilt was supposed to be yellow, do you?"

"I'm not sure. But yellow is a happy color, Mattie, so it must be all right."

"I guess yellow could be fine because red would mean danger. Right? Red always means danger, doesn't it?"

Martha looked at Jake's puzzled face.

"We're not supposed to move around in daylight, Jake, so we should probably wait here until it gets dark. Then maybe we'll remember the right color."

Jake looked unhappy. "But I don't see anyone around, Mattie, and it's not that far. I wanna go there."

Before she could stop him, Jake took off like a shot.

"Jake," she called, "I remember. It's blue. Blue's safe, not yellow!"

But he was too far away to hear her.

CHAPTER

12

MARTHA HELD her breath as Jake raced through the field, across the road and into the front yard. She heard a dog bark, and in a snap, Jake raced back across the road, through the field, and directly to his frantic sister.

"There's a big, huge, orange dog over there, Mattie. It barked at me and looked mean."

"Did you hear it growl?"

Martha sucked in her lips as Jake carefully thought this point over. "No, but it started coming toward me so I ran away as fast as I could."

"Maybe we should wait until it gets dark."

"No, Mattie," Jake whined. "I'm tired and I wanna go to that house."

Martha could see no way around this. If Jake had a fit, they were sunk. There was nothing here but that red farmhouse and nowhere else she knew to go. Yellow, red, or blue. It made no difference. She had to make a move now. So, she gathered herself together, stood as erect as she could on her uneven crutches, and put on a brave face.

"We'll have to go there, Jake, and face the dog. We have no choice. Pick up a few of those small rocks over there. Maybe we can chase it away and run for the front door." Jake did as he was told, and they headed off. Her heart pounding, Martha hobbled through the grassy weeds, keeping her ears and eyes alert to any strange sound or movement. All seemed quiet, even the dog. By the time they reached the road, the sun was shining brightly. Still, everything appeared safe.

As quickly as possible, Martha crossed the road to the front yard. There she and Jake were greeted not by a vicious monster but by a big, friendly golden-orange-haired dog wagging its tail a mile a minute.

Martha smiled in relief as Jake, fingering the stones he had gathered, tugged on her arm. "Make it go away, Mattie. I'm scared of it."

She enfolded his hand in hers. "She looks friendly, Jake. See her tail wagging? I think you can throw those stones away."

Meanwhile, the dog started barking and running back and forth between Martha and its doghouse further back in the yard. Martha stopped, not knowing what to do and somewhat fearful that maybe Jake had been right. She had never had a dog at home because of the runaway slaves. A dog might bark and frighten them, just as this one had, or worse, growl and snap at strangers on the property.

The dog came closer and, taking the bottom of Martha's dress in its mouth, started tugging her toward the doghouse.

"Mattie," Jake whimpered, "it's trying to bite you."

Martha straightened her back and stood her ground.

The creature was not growling or baring its teeth. Instead, it kept barking and running back and forth and then tugging on Martha. In the distance, Martha caught the sound of horses' hooves.

"I know this sounds peculiar, Jake, but I think the dog wants us to hide in her doghouse."

Gingerly, Martha hurried Jake over to the structure. It sure was bigger than any doghouse she had ever seen, and its entrance was higher and rounder.

Hearing the horses coming closer, she told Jake to lean over and get inside. "Go to the back and be really, really quiet."

Before she got down on her hands and knees to follow him, she tossed her crutches away. The dog chased after them, bringing the smaller one back to her. Jake stuck his head out of the doghouse to see what was going on.

"It wants to play fetch," he said, scrambling out and grabbing the end of the crutch. The dog pulled from its end.

"Oh, no," he laughed. "Now it's playing tug."

The horses were just around the bend of the road, and Martha had to act quickly.

"Jake," she ordered him, "just drop the thing and get into the doghouse."

Jake hurried inside and Martha dropped to her knees and crawled in after him. The doggy smell of it was almost overwhelming, and it was pitch black except for the opening, which was now almost totally covered by the panting dog. Martha turned her body and huddled next to Jake, hoping the slave catchers would not connect the tree branches with crutches.

Immediately after they settled in, the dog entered the doghouse, made a turn, and lay down with its head and paws sticking out into the sun. It remained totally alert, barking out from time to time.

Every few moments, its wagging tail swept across Jake's face, threatening to make him giggle. Martha shushed him as she heard the horses turn into the yard. It sounded like there were at least two of them. Her blood turned to ice as she also heard the braying of the bloodhounds. The golden dog stood up and growled. Jake wrapped both arms around Martha and whimpered.

"Hello there, boys," came a woman's voice and the sound of the farmhouse door opening and banging closed. "What brings you around here?"

"More than just our usual slave patrol, Miz Holden. We're looking for two runaways. The dogs brought us right here to your door."

Martha thought she recognized the voice as that of Will, but she was not absolutely sure. She gritted her teeth in anger and fright. Then she heard the woman, the one Lucy had told her about.

"Now you boys know I don't cotton with no runaways."

"We're just checkin' anyway, ma'am. Thought you might've seen them. Two young 'uns. Maybe fourteen and around seven. A girl and a boy."

"Young 'uns on their own? Should be easy to catch, but no, 'taint seen 'em." She paused for just a second, then added brightly, "Thought you boys might be hungry as usual."

"We sure are, ma'am. What've you got today?"

The woman's footsteps took her to the door, which

she opened. "Thanks, Samantha." Martha heard the door close again and the woman walk close to the dog-house where the dog still stood growling.

"You know how Samantha's afraid of the dogs, so she won't come out. But here, she made you some fresh cornbread and here's a few pieces of meat for the dogs and one for you, too, Rosie."

Martha saw a thin elderly white woman bend down, catch a quick glimpse of the inside of the doghouse, and give the dog the piece of meat. Then she stood up and threw the other pieces to the hounds. They gulped the meat down and brayed in a less threatening manner.

"Thanks, ma'am. We'll be off then. Keep this description and let us know if you see 'em. We'll be by tomorrow as usual."

Martha heard the men leave. For several minutes, nothing happened. Then the woman's head appeared in the doghouse entrance.

"We need to wait a good hour before I can move you. 'Til I know it's safe. Meanwhile, keep real quiet. Rosie here'll watch over you."

As if on cue, Rosie turned around so her big golden-orange head faced them, and then gave Martha and Jake each a big lick on the face. Jake giggled, but Martha merely wiped the slobber off with her arm. Rosie turned around again, exited the doghouse, and lay down in front of it keeping watch. Martha was so relieved that she endured the discomfort and nauseating smell without any complaints.

About an hour later, Miss Holden returned and peered at Martha, who squirmed at her displeased look. "Didn't you see the yellow quilt on the line?"

"Yes, ma'am, but I only heard about blue and got confused when I saw the yellow."

"Well, you didn't see blue, did you? Yellow means extreme caution. This is an important rule if you're gonna run away. Remember everything you're told, and if you're not sure about a thing, then you don't take no chances."

Martha was in no mood to hear another rule of the Underground Railroad and was impatient to be released from this dog cave.

"Can we come out of this smelly doghouse?" she asked.

"Smelly it might be, but it's saved many a runaway's life. And, yes, you can come out now, but quickly."

Martha pushed Jake out first. Miss Holden hurried him into the house and returned for Martha, who could barely stand. The older woman wrapped her arm around her and helped her along.

"What happened to you, child? This is bad, bad news for your escape."

"I sprained my ankle on some rocks crossing the river. I'm sure it'll be all right if I can just get my shoe off."

Once inside, Miss Holden introduced Martha and Jake to Samantha, a dark brown woman about half Miss Holden's age.

"How can you aid slaves, ma'am," Martha could not help asking, "if you own one?"

"I'm no slave," Samantha said.

"Indeed," Miss Holden added. "Samantha was once a slave, but I bought her and set her free, but that isn't any of your concern, is it now."

"No, ma'am. But I'm curious. Why doesn't Samantha go north where there isn't any slavery?"

"Because I like it here," Samantha harrumphed as she gently led Jake away for a bath and a change into clean clothes. "I think I have some shoes for you as well, boy," she told him.

Martha's own shoe presented a painful problem. To get it off, Miss Holden had to cut it away, and Martha winced with each cut and tug until her red and swollen foot emerged.

Miss Holden clucked her tongue. "Let's get you bathed and in clean clothes. Then I'll wrap your foot. I think I have a large-size shoe you can put over it. It'll have to do for now. And I'll replait your hair for you, too. Would you like that?"

Martha nodded consent as she thought of the many times her mama had done the same. She loved the gentle touch of her hands as she worked the long strands into two neat plaits. Meanwhile, Miss Holden continued, "We need to get the two of you away quickly, at least by this evening. It's too dangerous here. Look."

She handed Martha a sheet of paper with the following notice printed on it:

FIVE HUNDRED DOLLARS REWARD.
RAN AWAY.
TWO NEGROES
NAMED AS FOLLOWS:
MARTHA, AGED ABOUT 14 YEARS,
VERY LIGHT SKIN, ALMOST INDIAN LOOKING,
ABOUT 5 FEET 2 INCHES HEIGHT, FLESHY,
LONG STRAIGHT BLACK HAIR WORN
IN PLAITS AND BROWN EYES.
JAKE, AGED ABOUT SEVEN,

ALSO LIGHT SKINNED,
ALMOND-SHAPED HAZEL EYES
AND BLACK CURLY HAIR.

TWO HUNDRED AND FIFTY DOLLARS REWARD WILL
BE GIVEN FOR EACH OF THE ABOVE-NAMED NEGROES,
IF TAKEN OUT OF THE STATE,
AND TWO HUNDRED DOLLARS EACH IF TAKEN IN
THE STATE. THEY MUST BE LODGED IN BALTIMORE,
EASTON, OR CAMBRIDGE JAIL IN MARYLAND.

It was signed by Robert Dawes.

Martha wrinkled her brow, squinted her eyes, and clenched her fists. How could Robert Dawes make such a wild claim? She handed the notice back to Miss Holden. It was not a remembrance she cared to keep.

"We'll be ready to leave as soon as you say," she said.

"First a good bath. Second, a good meal. Third will be getting you ready for the next leg of your journey."

"Are we still in Maryland?"

"Yes. Near Denton."

Martha had no idea where that was.

"Tomorrow, you travel up into Delaware near Dover."

She remembered Dover, Delaware, from the maps she had studied at home. It was indeed in the right direction, and she was confident they would soon be home now that they were in the capable hands of conductors and stationmasters of the Underground Railroad. Never was Martha so happy to be in the care of responsible adults.

As she and Jake admired each other's clean clothes,

Martha heard the jingle of bells as a peddler's wagon pulled into the yard.

"Your train has arrived," said Miss Holden.

Martha peeked between the curtains to look at the vehicle that would carry her and Jake one step closer to Connecticut and home. There in front of the house stood a colorful wagon with pots and pans hanging from nails on its sides, knickknacks of all sorts dangling next to them, and a huge, brightly painted sign in beautiful cursive letters that said: "Solomon Giuseppe, Entrepreneur. Modern Household Conveniences, Fabrics, Decorative Items, and Medicines to Cure All That Ails You."

Martha heard Miss Holden next to her. "Samantha, please ask Solomon to lodge the wagon at the back of the house so no one can see us load our packages."

"Right away."

"What packages is he taking, Miss Holden?" she asked.

"You and Jake."

Solomon Giuseppe did what was requested and then entered the house, giving Samantha a big hug and kiss and Miss Holden a courteous nod. Martha's shock showed.

"They're married," Miss Holden whispered in her ear. "He comes home when he can, but he feels safer when he's away that Samantha's with me."

Martha took a sly look in Solomon Giuseppe's direction. He was deeply tanned and had a big bushy mustache that, she thought, must have tickled Samantha when he kissed her. He was also on the stocky side, but so tall that he did not appear obese. His hair was very dark and wavy and his deep brown eyes twinkled as he came up to her.

"Miss Martha, I presume from the notices I've been seeing posted along the road."

For some reason she did not understand, Martha felt shy. "Yes, sir."

"Please call me Solomon. And where is little Jake?"

Jake popped up from where he had been hiding behind the sofa. Martha saw his wariness, but somehow his curiosity got the better of him. Just as Solomon strode across the room with his hand out to shake Jake's, Miss Holden interrupted.

"Let's have a bite to eat so that as soon as the sun sets, we can load up and you'll be on your way."

"Won't the slave patrols wonder why a peddler is traveling by night?" asked Martha.

"I often travel at night so I can reach my next destination by daybreak. The patrols know me, and for some reason trust me," grinned Solomon.

Dinner was light, but delicious to the two hungry so-called runaways. Cold chicken, corn bread, and fresh tomatoes. Throughout it, Martha could not help staring at Solomon. Hadn't her parents told her that her birth father might have been a peddler? One that was maybe Afric or Italian?

Again, she could not stop herself from asking questions. She figured that if the questions were not about the Underground Railroad, no one would object. So she burst forth with an abundance of them.

"Solomon, have you been a peddler for long?"

"I would say about sixteen years, now."

Sixteen years, thought Martha. That fit within the time she was born.

"Have you ever peddled up North?"

"Sure have."

"To Connecticut?"

"For certain. I used to like New England summers. They're cooler than down here." He turned to Samantha and gently touched her cheek. "But now I don't like to go so far away from my lovely wife."

Martha could not care less about Samantha. She only wanted to know about Solomon. "Have you ever traveled with any Indians?"

Martha saw him hesitate. "What a strange question. Why do you ask?"

"I was just curious. I heard that sometimes peddlers travel with Indians that have no home and I've never seen an Indian and I was wondering what they're like. Especially what the women are like."

Martha saw Solomon cast a quick glance Samantha's way. "Can't say that I've ever traveled with no Indian. I just visit them sometimes to sell items. A customer's a customer, after all."

With that, he abruptly pushed himself away from the table, and said, "Time to start packing up."

Martha and Jake had nothing to carry, just her small bag with the knife and the leftover pieces of rope, and Jake's carved horse and her embroidered handkerchief, which she had carefully placed in the pocket of her new dress. She planned to give Jake the horse when he grew restless. With Jake in tow, she followed Miss Holden and Samantha out the back door to the wagon, where Solomon had removed a fake covering over the bottom of the inside and placed a quilt and two pillows in the space. How inventive it all was.

"I usually don't have room for blankets and pillows

for my cargo," he said, "but you two are smaller than my usual passengers. Maybe these will help to make the ride more comfortable."

Jake balked at being placed in the bottom of the wagon.

"I'm coming in next to you, Jakey," Martha said. "We'll be riding together."

He whimpered some, but allowed Solomon to lift him up and then help him to lie down. Then he took Martha aside.

"I noticed that your brother is somewhat jittery," he said. He then handed Martha a piece of candy wrapped in paper. "If he can't control himself and it looks like he'll put us all in danger, give him this. It's laced with laudanum and will put him to sleep."

Martha's forehead creased with concern. "Isn't that dangerous?"

"There's only enough to help him sleep for a few hours. Our journey'll take a good part of the night. I promise I wouldn't give you enough to harm him."

Martha slipped the laudanum-laced candy into her pocket, allowed Solomon to help her up into the wagon, and then lay down next to Jake. He moaned as Solomon placed the phony floorboard back above them and their world turned dark.

"I can't breathe, Mattie."

"Don't fret, Jake. Look to the side and you'll see little spaces in the wood to let air in and even some light. It's almost bedtime, anyway, and this'll be just like going to sleep at home. We'll sleep and in the morning we'll be much closer to Mama and Papa than we are now."

But Martha, too, could feel the suffocating darkness

around her, and it took all her inner strength not to panic. The space was small, too small, she thought, for a man or a family to hide in. How did they survive? While neither she nor Jake would be able to move around, it might be possible for them to turn just a little bit to ease their bones and stretch their muscles.

Martha felt the wagon rock as Solomon climbed up to his seat. He gave a small clucking sound, and the horse started slowly down the road. Martha could feel every bump, every sway, every stop and start, but soon a steady rhythm from the horse's hooves settled her nerves.

Jake, however, was having a bad time of it. Martha stroked his hair and ran her hand gently over his body. "Relax, Jake."

Then from her pocket she took the small carved horse. Feeling for his hand in the dark, she pressed it into his palm. "Here's your favorite little horse, Jakey. I've been holding it all this time to give to you. It carries Papa and Mama's love."

Jake wrapped the horse in his fist and continued to whimper. Martha soothed him some more by humming softly. Soon after, she heard Solomon sing in a low, deep voice:

Swing low, sweet chariot,
Comin' for to carry me home.
Swing low, sweet chariot,
Comin' for to carry me home.

As he continued singing, Martha felt Jake's body relax and his breathing slow. Before long, he was sound asleep. And, with thoughts of home and her papa singing the exact same song, so was she.

Martha awoke when she felt the wagon make a sharp turn and come to a stop. Dim light filtered through the cracks in the wood slats and she could hear two men speaking.

"What have you got here, Solomon?" a new voice said.

"Two small packages."

"Bring 'em back to the storehouse. We'll unload there."

The wagon moved again, stopped, and Martha heard the closing of large doors. Quickly Solomon's smiling face appeared as he lifted the phony floorboard and helped Martha and Jake out. "Welcome to Dover, Delaware. Next stop, Wilmington."

Somewhat embarrassed, Martha immediately asked if there was a privy for Jake, and the new man, whom Martha was told to call Daniel—just Daniel—led him over to a chamber pot behind a stack of hay.

"When do we leave, Solomon?" she asked.

"As soon as we get some food into you, let you stretch your legs a bit, use the privy, and settle you into your next conveyance."

"Where is it?"

"Over there." Martha saw a hay wagon waiting in the corner.

"My uncle and papa use hay wagons, too," she said.

"Don't tell me such things, child," he said gently. "It can be dangerous."

"I know," she responded. "But I always forget."

"Don't you fret, sweet Martha. You're doing a brave thing for a young girl. Coming all this way to get your brother. Your parents must be very proud of you."

This was her opportunity, Martha thought. Was Solomon hinting that he could be her father? As she opened her mouth again, Jake came running back and took hold of her hand. The moment had passed.

After about thirty minutes, Solomon and Daniel took Martha and Jake to the hay wagon. Before helping them up, Solomon reached into his pocket.

"Jake, my brave boy. Here's a gift for you." He handed Jake a small top. "When you get back home, you can play with this with your friends."

Martha could not tell Solomon that Jake did not have any friends. He had led as secret a life as any member of the Underground Railroad, and in school he had never been able to communicate well with other children. Maybe that had been for the best. A secret as great as his might have been almost impossible for him to keep.

"And for you, Martha, a little keepsake." Solomon then gave Martha a small wooden doll that fit into the palm of her hand. It was an Indian girl with a painted face, painted black braids just like Martha's, and a little white deerskin dress with beading on it.

Martha stared at it and then up into Solomon's face. "I'll never forget you, Solomon."

"And I won't forget you either, you darling child. Now," he coughed, "do you still have that piece of candy I gave you?"

"Yes."

"We gotta hurry," Daniel interjected. "There's no time to waste for these passengers."

Solomon gently lifted Martha and then Jake into the wagon. The top was secured, the darkness descended, and Martha heard stacks of hay being tossed on top of them. The door to the storehouse opened, and once again she felt the horses' hoofbeats, the swaying of the wagon, the ruts and bumps, and, all too soon, Jake's persistent bouncing on his back and legs and his arms twitching. Although it pained her to do it, she took the piece of candy and offered it to him. Again, she soothed his hair and stroked his arms and chest, and he calmed, drifting off to sleep as the laudanum took effect.

CHAPTER

13

MARTHA COULD not sleep. She tried to keep her eyes closed, but they popped open as if on a puppet's string. Small rays of sunshine filtering through the thin airholes of the wagon distracted her, and soon she regretted longing to feel the sun's warmth. Within an hour, the heat in the confined space drenched her in sweat. Dust from the hay tickled her nose, and several times she had to hold her breath until the need to sneeze subsided.

Her anxiety grew as her thoughts turned involuntarily to Caleb. Did he think about her? Did he wish he had not uttered those cruel words the night she told him her parents' secret about her birth? She could still see his shocked expression and the slight recoil of his body as she moved near him. One worry turned into another, this time about herself. Was she still plain old Martha, the same Martha she had always been? And Jake? Was he still the same person he had been? Would any of them be the same after this?

Her thoughts were interrupted abruptly when she heard the sound of galloping horses and men's shouts, and then felt the hay wagon come to a stop. Will and Tom, she shuddered. Why didn't they just leave her alone? She had never done anything to hurt them, so why did they want to hurt her?

"What is it you want?" she heard Daniel ask.

"Slave patrol. We're looking for two children. Runaways."

"Children? By themselves? How could that be?"

"With a little help from their friends." The slave catchers' voices came closer to the wagon and Martha instinctively tensed her body and prepared to cover Jake's mouth if he should mutter in his sleep. "Now, get down and unload the wagon."

Daniel spoke in a calm and quiet manner. "Sirs, this is a lot of hay. It'll take me hours to unload it. But if you wanna wait, so be it." He rocked the wagon as he slowly got down from his seat, lifted out his pitchfork, and stabbed a bale of hay.

Sweat ran down Martha's face as she strained to hear what would happen next. Will's voice came closer as if he was about to look through the slats and discover her lying there. "You're too slow, and we don't have time to wait. Gimme that pitchfork, and I'll just poke it around and see if I find anything."

Martha stiffened and tried to pull her body deeper down into the wagon. The prongs of a pitchfork came through several of the openings, once so close to her chest that she could see the hickory wood tines in the dim light. Thank goodness Jake was sound asleep. After several unbearable minutes, the prongs disappeared.

"Drat. Nothing there," Will complained. "C'mon, Tom, we're wasting time again."

Martha sighed in relief at the creaking of their leather saddles as they mounted their horses and galloped off. Soon, the wagon bounced as bales of hay were returned to their place. A whispering voice asked, "You all right?"

She forced out a "yes" as her body relaxed and her nerves and muscles buzzed.

Hours later, the hay wagon arrived in Wilmington, Delaware. After Daniel removed the hay and the false cover, Martha jumped to her freedom, wincing as her ankle gave an angry twinge. She immediately reached for Jake, who was still groggy from the laudanum, and then looked around for their next conveyance. All she saw was a wagon with a pile of bricks next to it. Surely, this could not be it. But it was.

"We're traveling again tonight, Jake, so you can sleep more, and then tomorrow, we'll be in the North," she said.

For a moment, his eyes lit up. "Will Mama and Papa be there?"

Martha's eyes teared up. "Not yet, but in a couple of days."

Martha was more fearful of being under a wagon full of bricks than of any of the other loads. What if the fake bottom gave out and the rocks fell on top of them? But there was no choice. Jake quickly nodded off while Martha dozed, feeling no joy in the sound of the slow-moving wagon.

Toward daybreak, Martha felt the team make a sharp turn and pull off the road. She heard brick after brick being unloaded, and then a bright female voice said, "Welcome to Chester County, Pennsylvania. Thee has reached freedom."

What a great relief to be in the North and also to hear the familiar Quaker plain speech. Yet, Martha also felt a flash of anger at people assuming they were runaways.

"But we are free already," she blurted out. "Always have been."

"Ah," said the woman as she brushed dirt from Martha's dress, "so thee is the famous Martha. I was told thee is outspoken."

Martha blushed and helped the woman brush down Jake, who looked a bit more awake than he had yesterday.

"I'm Thelma. My husband, Nathaniel, will soon carry thee to Philadelphia in our milk wagon. Thee can sit in the back hidden from view."

Thelma took Martha and Jake inside her simple but comfortable home for some real food. After almost two days of a bite here and there, they were famished and gobbled up eggs, biscuits, ham, and sweet rolls—made with honey, of course. Like her own mama, she was sure that Thelma would not use slave-grown sugar to bake her pastries.

"Thelma," Martha began, "what will happen to us next?"

"The Philadelphia Anti-Slavery Society members are awaiting thee. They'll prepare thee for thy next stop. But we must hurry. We're all aware that there're several slave catchers looking everywhere for thee."

"Several?" Martha asked. "I thought there were only two."

"I'm afraid not. The reward is substantial, you know.

Four or five have already been to Philadelphia, but, of course, they didn't find thee. It's good they're one step ahead of thee, although they do often backtrack. That's why we move quickly and use back roads and private conveyances."

Martha's heart began the now-familiar pounding it did every time she thought of Will and Tom. And now there were others as well. "Can we go around Philadelphia? Directly to Connecticut?"

Thelma's lips puckered. "I can't discuss plans, Martha. In fact, I really don't know them. Now, let's hurry."

In a short while, Martha and Jake found themselves in an empty space in the back of the milk wagon behind two huge tin vats of milk and under some smelly rounds of cheese. As the wagon took off at a steady clip-clop, Jake entertained himself with his horse and by examining his top. Martha felt in her pocket for her Indian doll and her embroidered handkerchief, but she did not take them out for fear of losing them.

Philadelphia was just as Martha remembered it. The smoke and dirt and smells from her last trip seemed even stronger. Jake was both alarmed and fascinated by the place. It took all her energy to keep him from trying to climb into the front of the wagon to gaze out at the sights.

"I'll take you on a trip to Philadelphia when I'm eighteen and you're twelve. How about that?"

"Will we have to hide to get there?"

"Absolutely not. We'll take a train and a boat. Maybe by then, we'll be able to take a train the whole way. Would you like that?"

"I saw a picture of a train once, Mattie. I'd like to ride in one. That'd be fun."

"Silence, please," came a stern voice from the front.

Martha merely smiled. She could see Liberty Falls in her mind and imagine her mama and papa and Caleb and Becky and Adam Burke waiting for her. They would throw her a big celebration for bringing Jake safely home.

Sooner than she expected, members of the Anti-Slavery Society greeted her and Jake warmly in the home of one of its members. A smiling young black woman took Jake by the hand and led him off to the kitchen. He trusted her immediately, barely taking a moment to look back at Martha.

"We were hoping to keep you here for a while so you could rest and clean up," said one woman, whose name Martha did not even have time to learn, "but it's urgent that we move you on to New York."

Martha grinned. "And from there it's just two days from our home in Connecticut, isn't it?"

The woman looked at Martha sadly. "You won't be going home, I'm afraid. It's too dangerous. Robert Dawes is determined to find you and Jake and so we're sending you on to Canada."

Martha was startled, confused, heartbroken. "Canada?"

"Yes, it's all arranged. You leave in just a few minutes in a private carriage for New Jersey, then a ferry to New York. Just outside the city, you'll need to change into these clothes I have for you. You'll dress in boys' clothes and Jake in girls'. You'll then take a train with a group of white abolitionists heading for a meeting in Buffalo. Then our Canadian friends will guide you over to a place where you'll be safe. We believe it's most prudent that for this part of your trip you both be considered white."

Once again, Martha was puzzled by the confusing race issue. Did this woman believe she was colored? Was she? "I don't understand," she said.

"Well, your coloring allows you to look white when you need to. It'll be more difficult for the slave catchers to identify you if you're surrounded by whites. They usually aren't too clever, and we've been able to fool them in any number of ways. Everything'll happen very quickly, so you must be ready."

She handed Martha a small satchel. "The clothes are inside. Dress, bonnet, slippers, stockings for Jake. Pants, shirt, jacket, boots for you."

"But Jake'll never allow me to dress him in girls' clothes."

"He must. And, Martha, to prepare, you'll have to cut your hair to look like a boy's."

Of all the things she had been asked to do during her journey, this was the most difficult. Martha's mother had snipped the ends off her hair every now and then so as to make them look neat, but otherwise, she had never cut her hair. She ran her hand through it with great love and sorrow, being sure to give her plaits a few affectionate twists.

"Now is not the time for self-pride," ordered the woman. "Here, let me cut it." Within a moment, Martha felt the scissors hack off each of her braids. The woman then snipped here and there to even the ends. Tears streamed down Martha's face.

"Would you send the plaits to my mama and papa as a keepsake?" she asked.

The woman glanced away as tears filled her own eyes. "Yes, of course."

When Jake rejoined Martha, he simply stared at her. "Why did you cut off your hair, Mattie?"

"I'll explain later, Jake." How was she ever going to convince him to dress as a girl?

The carriage from Philadelphia moved quickly even though it was night. Two lanterns and a nearly full moon helpfully lit the way. When they came near the ferry that connected New Jersey to New York, the carriage pulled off the road so Martha and Jake could prepare themselves for the final leg of their journey. Martha put an arm around Jake, looked into his face, and presented her proposal.

"Jake, we're gonna have to play a game to make this last part of our journey."

"I like games, Mattie."

"Good. In this one, I'm gonna pretend I'm a boy, and you're gonna pretend you're a girl."

Jake grimaced. "I don't like that idea, Mattie."

"I know, but we have to do it because we don't want the slave catchers to find us. But you know what's the best part?"

"What?"

"We're gonna take a train. And we're gonna sit in real seats."

He grinned excitedly. "A train? Sitting in real seats? I like that. It's way better than those wagons, right?"

"Uh-huh. So will you play the game?"

Martha tickled Jake under his arms to make him laugh. He had such a nice hopeful view of things, she thought. "Will you?"

"Okay, Mattie. But just for a little while."

Martha helped Jake change into the girls' clothes. The result was incredible. He certainly looked like a little girl even with the ugly frown on his face.

"These clothes itch and scratch. And how will I walk in these skirts?" Martha laughed as he strode forward and promptly stumbled.

"You won't have to walk much. We'll be on the train."

Martha then quickly changed her clothes. What freedom she felt! The pants were roomy and the jacket warm and comfortable, even if the shirt's collar was a bit stiff. The boots felt much sturdier than her usual shoes and helped to support her still-sore ankle. The cap allowed her to see much better than a bonnet like the one Jake was pushing around his head that very moment.

With their new identities, Martha and Jake climbed back into the carriage. Early in the evening, they reached a massive depot on New York's Hudson River shore. There they were passed over to a group of white abolitionists, both men and women. The women scooped up Jake and led him to the steep steps into the train. He looked nervously back at Martha but she just smiled encouragingly at him. A family with three young daughters between Jake's age and her own took him to be with them.

Then the men led her up the same steps and seated her across the aisle a few rows behind Jake. He kept turning around to stare at her, but each time, she signaled him to turn around.

The young man sitting next to her introduced himself as Fred Jenkins of Yonkers, New York. "And you are Matthew, I hear," he said.

Martha stalled for a brief second and answered in a deepened voice, "Yes. I'm Matthew from, um, Brooklyn."

Fred laughed kindly. "You can speak normally. No one will hear but us abolitionists. Anyway, we'll be leaving soon. This train'll take us to Albany."

Martha smiled, her face hot with embarrassment. "How long will it take?"

"Maybe four hours. Then we'll switch trains and travel through the night to Buffalo."

"I understand."

For Martha, the journey was full of tension and worry. From time to time, she saw Jake swaying back and forth or bobbing up and down or turning his head to make sure she was still there. Every time she saw him in distress, she also noticed that the family he was with diverted his attention. They gave him something to eat or pulled out a toy. At one point, the older girl, the one who seemed close in age to Martha herself, started to read to him from a large picture book version of *Uncle Tom's Cabin*. From time to time, Jake nodded off, but Martha sat upright, alert to any problems that might come their way.

All went smoothly, including the transfer from one train to another in Albany. Then, as they entered Buffalo, the train came to a halt. The conductor entered.

"Folks," he said in a disgusted voice, "before we disembark, some officials insist on going through the car reserved for coloreds, checking for freedmen's papers."

A chill ran up Martha's spine, and she shivered. Fred Jenkins moved an inch closer and patted her arm in a distinctly manly way. "Don't fret, Matthew, we won't miss our meeting."

Ten minutes passed. Nothing happened. Fifteen minutes. Twenty. Martha peered out the window and saw two rough-looking men arguing with the conductor. Will and Tom. She would know them anywhere. Finally, the conductor threw up his arms and climbed up the steps to her car, the leering men following him.

"Folks," he announced, "these deputies have insisted on searching this car. They have reason to suspect that two runaways are pretending to be white."

Will pushed him aside and stood boldly at the front of the car. Jake immediately jumped up. "Mattie!"

Will moved swiftly to grab hold of him, but not fast enough. As Jake crouched down behind the seat in front of him, Martha bent over to the sack Lucy had given her. For some reason, she had never left it behind. Now, she took out the knife and quickly unwrapped it. Will, meanwhile, succeeded in grabbing Jake. He shook him and shouted in his face, "You're comin' with me."

Martha saw Jake straining away, frightened and angry but not saying a word. Her own fury exploded as she rushed forward with the knife held outright in her hand.

In a strong quiet voice, she pointed it directly at Will's chest. "Let him go."

"Ah, Martha," he replied. "I knew you were here. Now, you'd make everything very simple for Jake and all these folk if you'd just drop the knife. Mr. Dawes has no interest in you if we bring him the boy. I take him and then you can go home to your mama and papa. You refuse, and then Mr. Dawes will be *very* interested in a little bit of revenge."

Martha shivered with fright, but she did not move an inch. Everyone else in the car seemed frozen in place. Do something, Martha thought. Why don't they do something?

Will coaxed some more. "C'mon, Martha. Don't you wanna go home? Canada'll be a cold and lonely place for you without your mama and papa to take care of you."

Martha was boiling. Not shy. Not afraid. From somewhere deep inside, she felt a surge of strength. She lunged forward, but Will was the stronger. He grabbed her hand and struggled with her. The knife clattered to the floor.

"Tom, help me with the boy, and let's get outta here," he called to his friend. But the passengers sitting in the very front of the car had gotten up and pushed Tom back out the door. They now turned their attention to Will.

The young girl who had been reading to Jake took her large picture book and slammed it against Will's arm. The smallest girl kicked him in the leg. The third jumped up and down, trying to knock him on the head with her purse. Although he winced with each blow, he did not let go of his two captives. Martha looked at Jake struggling to get away from Will, and with new-found determination she bent over and bit Will's hand. Jake, following her lead, did the same.

At that moment, the rest of the passengers rose as one. Fists started flying. People pushed and shoved. Many yelled at Will and the conductor.

"You let those children go."

"Arrest this kidnapping abomination."

"Get the other one, too, before he gets away."

"Conductor, let us out of this here train."

In all the melee, Martha and Jake struggled with Will, kicking, biting, hitting, doing anything they could to get him away from them. Just as Martha felt Will's grasp on them loosening, out of nowhere, a fist came flying at her face. She fell backward, hitting her head against the metal of the seat behind her, and the world turned black.

14

HOURS LATER, Martha woke up disoriented and confused. At first, she thought she was home, but she soon realized this was not the same parlor she grew up in. Besides that, something was wrong with her memory. She had no idea what had happened to her, where she was, or why her body ached so. The letter she found on the table from her papa and the thoughts that it triggered brought back her memory.

Just as her panic to find out what had happened to Jake pushed her up onto her wobbling legs, the parlor door opened and a small black woman of about her mama's age walked in, followed by a not-so-tall stout black man in a minister's suit.

The woman spoke in warm, soothing tones. "Good morning, Martha, dear. Are you feeling better?"

"Where am I? And who are you?"

The couple came closer, the woman gently encircling Martha's waist with her right arm. She helped her to sit down, taking the seat next to her without letting go of her comforting embrace.

"I'm Fanny Thompson and this is my husband, Abijah. Most folks around here call him Reverend. And you're in Aramintaville, Canada."

"Canada." Martha paused. She shivered involuntarily as thoughts of the slave catchers flashed through her mind. With growing alarm, she asked, "What about Jake? Did they take him?"

"No, they didn't. You put up such a good fight that you raised a rescue right there on the train. He's fine."

"Oh, thank goodness! Where is he? I need to see him."

"In a few minutes, dear. He's having something to eat. In fact, I'll go now to see if he needs anything." Releasing her hold on Martha, she quietly left the room. Her husband then sat down in the place she had vacated.

Martha again ran her hand over her throbbing head and gingerly touched her aching eye. She longed to go to sleep, but refused to lie back down. She needed to know that Jake was truly here in this house with her and that he was unharmed. She longed to hold him in her arms and feel his wonderfully strong, sturdy, innocent presence.

"Martha," Reverend Thompson said, "are you all right?"

"Yes, Reverend Thompson. Just thinking and remembering."

"I understand. Do you want to tell me about it?"

For a few moments, a comfortable silence filled the room. Then Martha began talking, and once she started, she could not stop. Words tumbled from her mouth as she reconstructed her past. She told the reverend about how Jake had entered her life almost eight years ago. His birth. How she took care of him. The slave catchers always, always coming to look for him. The abominable Fugitive Slave Law. Dawes kidnapping Jake. Her mama's breakdown. The revelation of her race. Her papa. Caleb. Becky. And the rescue on the Underground Railroad.

When she finished, Reverend Thompson took her shaking hands into his large warm ones and squeezed them gently. "You've been through a great deal, child," he said.

"Yes, I have," she replied. She wanted to tell him more and to ask him questions about how to live in a country that was unkind to people who were not white. And about Jake, who still believed he was a white child who had been abducted into slavery. She truly believed that the sooner he knew about his own identity, the better. That his natural mother was the runaway slave Mariah, and his father, Robert Dawes. And she had to tell him about herself as well. There must be no more lies. Lies had hurt them both, and they could only find their place in the world if they always knew the truth.

"Can I see Jake now?" she pleaded.

"I think it's good that we spoke beforehand. There's just one more thing, though."

Martha shifted in her seat and prepared to stand up.

"I'm very anxious to see him. He really needs me."

"Yes, he does. But he's a strong little boy and is in fine hands. My wife is very good with children. We had six of our own," he added, "but we lost each one to slavery."

Martha felt her face turn red with shame and

embarrassment, but the reverend's kind face put her at ease.

"Now," he said, patting her arm. "That one more thing I mentioned . . ."

"What is it?"

"You and Jake cannot return home until it's safe."

"How long will that be?"

"Maybe a couple of months. Think of this as a summer visit with friends. Can you do that?"

Martha bit her lip and mustered up her courage.

"I'll try. But I worry about my mama and papa."

"I understand, but you need to remain hopeful so that Jake feels safe and is not frightened. He's been through enough for such a young and innocent child."

Martha lowered her head and stared at her hands, which had begun shaking again. The future looked so scary that great big tears once again fell from her eyes. She took her handkerchief with the embroidered red rose and wiped them away.

"I'm sorry, Reverend," she managed to whisper.

He gently patted her on the shoulder. "No need to apologize, Martha. You've been through a terrible ordeal, but you're safe now and among friends."

Martha nodded and produced a small smile. "But I'm frightened and homesick. And where will Jake and I stay meanwhile?"

The reverend gave her his wonderfully big smile. "My wife and I hope you'll want to stay with us. We enjoy having young ones with us whenever we get the chance."

As Martha absorbed the reverend's words, a small head peeked into the room.

"Mattie!" Jake ran to her and wrapped his arms around her. "Are you better?"

She was so happy to see him that her eyes again welled up as she grabbed him and hugged him tightly for a good long time.

"I'll leave you two alone now," Reverend Thompson said as he raised himself from the chair and left the room, being careful to close the door behind him.

"I'm fine, Jakey. How are you?" Martha tickled him under his armpits to see him smile.

"I'm good. See? I have boys' clothes back. And I'm nice and clean. And I helped Aunt Fanny cook hot-cakes. I saved you some on the stove."

"That's good. I can't wait to taste them."

"Mattie. I like it here. But when can we go home?"

"Soon, I hope, but for now, we'll stay here. Mr. Dawes is still wanting to take you, I'm afraid. And he's real angry with me, too. Reverend Thompson asked if we'd like to spend the summer here with him and Mrs. Thompson. What do you think?"

"I guess we could. But just for a visit, right?"

"Right."

Martha and Jake gazed at each other, deep love and understanding passing between them. Then, Jake lowered his voice. "Are we safe here, Mattie?"

"Yes, Jake, we are."

"He can't take us away from here?"

"No, he can't."

Jake balled up his fists like a bare-knuckle prize-fighter. "Even if he tried, I'd fight him off like on the train."

Martha laughed. "Yes, indeed, you would."

Jake wrapped his arms once again around Martha's neck and leaned his cheek next to her ear. Then he said something she never thought she would hear from him.

"I love you, Mattie."

And she responded with something she never thought she would say to him.

"I love you, too, Jake."

After another long hug, Martha sat Jake down next to her. Now was the time to begin ridding themselves of the lies. "I have to tell you something, Jake. Something about yourself."

"You mean that I'm an Afric person? And that my first mama was Mariah and my first papa was that mean Mr. Dawes?"

Martha was shocked. "How did you know?"

"Granma Lucy told me. I didn't believe her for a long time. But now I do. It's nice, isn't it, Mattie? Being black *and* white?"

Martha laughed. "Well, I suppose it is. And you know what?"

"What?"

"I'm two colors, too. Maybe even more."

"You are? How did that happen?"

Martha told Jake her story. As he listened, he sucked his lips and shook his head from side to side. By the end, his eyes had grown as big as stars.

"But, you know, Jake. I think I've learned a lot about people on our journey. There are good people, not-so-good people, not-so-bad people, and bad people. I've come to think that what people look like really doesn't matter. As long as there are wonderful people like the ones who helped us out."

Jake nodded his head like he always did when he knew Martha was telling him something important. He did not really understand it all but he would think about it very hard. Finally, after several moments of silence, he patted her on the arm.

"I'm sorry you don't know who they are, though. Your mama and papa, I mean."

"My mama and papa are Sarah and Micah, the same as yours, Jake. They have always been our real mama and papa."

Jake nodded as Martha added, "Now, I'm famished. Where are those hotcakes you promised me?"

June turned into July and then August. Martha's papa sent short letters via the Underground Railroad, but to be safe he did not reveal any details. In the meantime, Martha and Jake's newly claimed Aunt Fanny and Uncle Abijah filled their lives with happiness and adventure. Aunt Fanny taught Jake about food. Every day she took him to the market-place or a local farm, where she helped him pick out new foods to taste. Together, they cooked every meal eaten in the house.

Martha spent her days with Uncle Abijah who, besides being a reverend, was something of a doctor. Martha went with him from house to house, learning how to cure illnesses and tend to injuries. She loved the work and thought she might like to become a doctor one day. She had read in *The Liberator* about Elizabeth Blackwell being the first woman back home to go to medical school, and the story gave Martha wonder-ful dreams of helping runaway slaves and poor people recover from illnesses and injuries. Maybe she would be the one to save another poor girl like Mariah from dying while giving birth to a freeborn child.

At the end of September, Aunt Fanny brought Martha and Jake a letter from the post office.

"See, dear ones," she said, "it's addressed to Martha and Jake Bartlett at our address."

Martha stared at their names.

"And," Aunt Fanny added, "there is a return address up here for Micah Bartlett in Liberty Falls, Connecticut."

Martha's face lit up. "Do you think this means what I think it does, Aunt Fanny? That it's safe back home?"

"It could be. Why don't you open it?"

Martha held the envelope for a brief moment, then tore it open and began reading.

"Read it aloud, Mattie," Jake demanded.

"Of course, Jake. Sorry."

"My dearest children," she began. *"I have very big and wonderful news."* Martha paused, her eyes poring over the words.

Jake leaned over her arm. "Go on, Mattie. Don't stop."

"Those abominable slave catchers, Will and Tom, have been arrested in Pomfret for kidnapping a free colored boy. It appears they got so frustrated by not finding you that they decided to make a little money by selling another poor soul into slavery. They snatched the boy just before he reached his school one morning. But, fortunately, he had forgotten his luncheon and his papa was on horseback to bring it to him. While he and his papa were fighting off the evil men, the Pomfret townspeople heard the ruckus and promptly rescued the boy and called the constable to arrest Will and Tom."

"Those wicked men," said Uncle Abijah, who had come in to hear the news.

Martha cleared her throat.

"*They are in the Brooklyn jail awaiting trial, but there is no doubt that they will be sent to prison for a very long time.*

"*Adam Burke told me that they had appealed to Robert Dawes for help, but he sent a most surprising letter to the court saying he does not condone the abduction of free children and that the court should do with Will and Tom as they see fit.*"

Martha looked up in surprise. "That's most odd, don't you think?"

"Mattie." Jake shook her arm. "Go. On."

Martha scanned the letter quickly. "Ah. This explains it. Listen, Jake. '*Adam Burke found out from Harriet Tubman that the truth is the other white plantation owners were so angry with Dawes for setting fire to Lorraine Perry's home and, hence, the rest of the town that they pressured him to forget about his search for you. They want peace, not the threat of slave revolts.*'"

"I'm sad about the fire," said Jake, "but I'm glad Mr. Dawes's friends have stopped him from scaring us."

Martha broke into a wide smile as she read on: "*So I write with great joy to say that it is once again safe for you in Liberty Falls. I will hurry to finish bringing in the harvest this week and then leave for Canada to bring you home. Caleb offered to go in my place, but this is one journey I wish to make myself. He can tend to the shop for a short while, and Aunt Edith will come to stay with your mama.*

"*I am eager to see you and hold you both in my arms. Expect me to arrive in a week or two.*"

Martha folded the letter and looked at Jake. "It's signed, '*Your loving father, Micah Bartlett.*'"

Jake turned to his new aunt and uncle.

"Mattie," he said, "can Aunt Fanny and Uncle Abijah come with us?"

"Jake," Uncle Abijah said, "that is the nicest thing anyone has ever said to us. But Aramintaville is our home, just like Liberty Falls is yours, and we have important work to do here. Besides, remember, we are runaway slaves. Here we are free. There we'd be in great danger."

Jake nodded, his face reflecting his newfound understanding of his world. Then, as quickly as his frown had appeared, it vanished, leaving a beautiful smile in its place.

"Can we come and visit you next summer?" he asked.

"Yes, indeed," Aunt Fanny answered. "We would like that very, very much. That is, if your mama and papa agree."

Two weeks later as Martha and Jake stood outside enjoying the last of the autumn warmth, they spotted a familiar figure walking up the street with a satchel in one hand.

"Papa!" Jake shouted. "Mattie, there's Papa."

Within the blink of an eye, he took off, running as fast as his almost-eight-year-old legs could carry him. Martha followed, nearly tripping over her skirt in her rush to reach him.

"Papa, Papa," she sobbed as she felt his arms enfold her. There they stood—Martha, Jake, and their papa—hugging and hugging. Martha could not tell if her face was wet from tears or kisses.

Once all the hugging and kissing were done, Martha forced out a sentence she could not hold back.

"Papa, you didn't mention Mama in your letters. How is she?"

"I am hopeful for her, Mahthah. Before I left home, I sat with her and told her about the slave catchers and Robert Dawes and said that I was coming to bring you home. For the first time in many months, she smiled that lovely smile of hers and said, 'Thank thee, Micah. Thank thee for bringing my babies home.' She will be waiting to embrace you."

"And what about Granma Lucy?" asked Jake.

"And Mrs. Perry," added Martha.

"I don't know," their papa replied. "Lucy is most likely still on the plantation. No one has heard from Mrs. Perry. Some say she fled town. Others that she perished in the fire."

There was silence for several seconds. Then Martha said, "And Papa, no more lies?"

"Never, Mahthah. I promise. No more lies."

Martha grinned and, with one arm looped through her papa's arm and the other holding Jake close, she led them to the house to meet a welcoming Aunt Fanny and Uncle Abijah.

Letter to the Reader

Dear Reader,

Martha and the Slave Catchers takes place during a time of turmoil in US history. The country was torn between two opposing sentiments: pro-slavery and anti-slavery. Tensions that were building during the 1830s and 1840s became worse with the passage of the Compromise of 1850, which incorporated a new version of the Fugitive Slave Law. From that point on, people living in free states were forced by law to participate in the capture and return of runaway slaves. As a result, the Underground Railroad and local Vigilance Committees worked all the harder to help fugitives reach a safe haven. No longer could those fugitives rely on the security of Northern states. Their freedom was not granted unless they reached Canada.

Since the beginning of the slave trade in the US, more than 100,000 enslaved people made attempts to free themselves. The majority of those were young, strong men who traveled alone. But there were also small groups and even families who made the run for freedom. If captured and returned, they faced torture, maiming, and possible death. In Martha's story, we learn about Jake's biological mother, Mariah, and her desperate attempt to free herself and her unborn child from the grip of Robert Dawes. Mariah arrived at Martha's aunt and uncle's home alone. How did she get there? Did she travel by herself? Did she have a guide? We never learn about her experience because she died before saying even one word about it.

Those fugitives who traveled through Philadelphia often met with the great abolitionist William Still, who recorded their experiences. They were not made public until 1872, when the stories could be safely told. You can find the book online at no cost. Look for *The Underground Railroad: A Record of Facts, Authentic Narrative, Letters, &c., Narrating the Hardships, Hair-breadth Escapes and Death Struggles of the Slaves in their efforts of Freedom, as Related by Themselves and Others, or Witnessed by the Author.* You will be amazed by the number of people who risked their lives on their journey to freedom.

The story of the Underground Railroad is an exciting one. My favorite book on the topic is Fergus M. Bordewich's *Bound for Canaan: The Epic Story of the Underground Railroad, America's First Civil Rights Movement* (2005). It gives a thorough view of the network of safe houses and routes that fugitives might have used to reach freedom up North. For Martha's story, I decided to center on the location and routes primarily used by Harriet Tubman, a woman I am sure that you have heard about in your classes or in books, movies, or TV shows. For solid information on Tubman's life and trips to Maryland to help free others, I relied on Kate Clifford Larson's *Bound for the Promised Land: Harriet Tubman, Portrait of an American Hero* (2004). It is a wonderful book. Both of these books on the Underground Railroad were written for adults, but I am sure that you would find the stories in them very exciting, clear, and readable.

For me, Martha and Jake are very much like the real people I wrote about in my adult book, *Growing Up Abolitionist: The Story of the Garrison Children* (2002). You see, I was very curious to know how people involved in the anti-slavery movement raised their children, so I spent ten years researching and writing about the family of William Lloyd Garrison, the anti-slavery leader responsible for the publication of the weekly newspaper *The Liberator*. I read thousands of personal letters from every member of the family, written to each other and to hundreds of other anti-slavery activists. I learned a great deal about how the parents taught their children to become the next generation of anti-slavery activists if slavery did not end in their own lifetimes.

Many of the details of Martha and Jake's lives are the same as those of real white and black abolitionist children in the 1800s, especially those who helped runaway slaves through the work of the Underground Railroad. Their home lives, the secrets they kept and, sometimes, the lies they heard and told, and their education through magazines, newspapers, and children's books were part of their childhood experiences. Their parents were their heroes, as were such great leaders as Harriet Tubman, who plays a key role in Martha and Jake's story. Abolitionist children were very aware of the dangers their role models faced to fight against slavery.

And as you saw in Martha and Jake's story, the Fugitive Slave Law of 1850, in particular, affected their safety and well-being. Martha, like many real abolitionist children, knew about the kidnapping of Northern children by slave catchers seeking to make an easy dollar from rewards for returning fugitives to slavery. Of course, it was easy for a slave owner to claim a person was a runaway if an individual even slightly resembled one of their former "possessions." So these slave catchers (or slave hunters as they were also called) snatched free children just walking along the road on their way to school or running an errand. It became dangerous for children of color to be out on their own. The examples I use in Martha's reading of the newspapers came from a booklet published by the American Anti-Slavery Society in 1856 called *Anti-Slavery Tracts, No. 18. The Fugitive Slave Law and Its Victims*. These were all real stories about real people, many of them children. I changed the dates of two of the stories to fit into my narrative, but the tales are still true. You can find this document free online if you want to read it for yourself.

Martha and the Slave Catchers contains a great many other facts. For example, even though Liberty Falls, LaGrange, and Aramintaville are figments of my imagination, all the other places are real. (Araminta Ross, by the way, was Harriet Tubman's original name.) Anti-slavery fairs were held each winter in several places as fund-raisers for the cause. Easily accessible online is *The Anti-Slavery Alphabet*, as well as other writings for abolitionist children. I introduce and explain other facts on my website: http://harrietalonso.com. Just go to the top of any page and click on *Martha and the Slave Catchers*.

Another thing I want to share with you is that I used language that was specific to the nineteenth century. Words like "plaits," "vexed," "conundrum," and many others were used at the time. Even expressions like "knee high to a bumblebee" and "you are some pumpkins" date from then. But you can easily understand these from the context.

I also use the words "colored," "Afric," and "Afric American" to describe African Americans. These were respectful terms of the time.

Martha's mother and Adam Burke use "Quaker Plain Speech" when they speak of "thee," "thou," "thy" and "thine." By the time Martha's story takes place, the use of these words was changing, and different groups of Quakers (or Friends as they were also called) used them in different ways. "Thee," in particular, became the pronoun of choice for both the subject and object in a sentence. I fashioned my usage after the style of Harriet Beecher Stowe in her best-selling 1852 novel, *Uncle Tom's Cabin*. Let me give you an example of what I mean. In Chapter XIII, "The Quaker Settlement," a Quaker woman says to the runaway slave Eliza, "And so thee still thinks of going to Canada, Eliza? . . . And what'll thee do, when thee gets there? Thee must think about that, my daughter." An adult's ear may want her to use the "thou" form they are more familiar with from Shakespeare and other writers—"thou still thinkest" and "what will thou doest . . . ?" But Quaker Plain Speech of the nineteenth-century US says otherwise. Jessamyn West, a popular contemporary Quaker author, saw her best-selling novel, *The Friendly Persuasion*, published in 1945. She, too, uses this form of Quaker Plain Speech. The novel is still so popular that it was reissued in 2003.

You may wonder why neither Martha nor Jake use Quaker Plain Speech. Part of the reason is that their father, who is not a Quaker, does not use it. The other is that many Quaker abolitionist children spoke in modern English as they lived within a diverse community.

I hope that you enjoyed reading *Martha and the Slave Catchers* as much as I enjoyed writing it. I am sure you have heard the expression "It takes a village to raise a child." Well, it also takes a lot of people to make a book. Although the story is mine, a number of people read it while I was writing it and made lots of good suggestions. I would like to thank them here.

First is my agent, Marie Brown of Marie Brown Associates. An agent is a person who finds a good publisher for her clients. But she does other things as well. Marie gave me good suggestions for improving the story and finding a publisher who would nourish it. I want to thank her from the bottom of my heart for her continued support and faith in Martha and Jake's story. And I also thank Eugene Nesmith and Michele Wallace for helping me to contact Marie.

The publisher is, of course, Seven Stories Press, and its president is Dan Simon. Triangle Square Books for Young Readers, the imprint of the press that publishes children's books, became Martha and Jake's (and my) home. I want to thank Dan, as well as the director of Triangle Square, Ruth Weiner, Lauren Hooker, and the rest of the staff for their care in seeing that Martha and Jake's story came to light. The dynamic illustrations that you see on the cover and in the pages of the book are the work of Elizabeth Zunon, and I thank her for bringing my imaginary people to life. The maps that help you to envision Martha's trip south and her and Jake's trip back north are the beautiful products of geographer Patricia Caro. I based these trips on the real-life journeys of two women who "stole" their freedom: Harriet Tubman and Ann Maria Weems. Finally, the curriculum guide designed to offer your teachers and parents some suggestions for sharing the book with you is thanks to Catherine Franklin, a wonderful professor of childhood education at the City College of New York.

Writers often take courses so they can learn from experts what makes a good story. I attended classes at the Gotham Writers Workshop and would like to thank my instructors, Michael Leviton and Margaret Meacham, for their helpful feedback on the early work I did. Maggie, in particular, stuck with the book through its completion and offered invaluable advice and support.

Writers often rely on other writers, colleagues, and friends to respond to their work. For me this included my writing group: Betsy Rorschak, Lizzie Ross, Laurin Grollin, Gail Gurland, and Joe Nagler, all accomplished writers. I also want to

246 MARTHA AND THE SLAVE CATCHERS

thank Deborah Anne McComb, Bonnie Anderson, Catherine Franklin, Mona Siegel, Anne Marie Pois, and Rebecca Johnson. And my youngest reader, Amelie Ingram, was a very special reader for me. A special thanks goes to the City College of New York history department for a small grant which allowed Lydia Shestopalova to conduct research in *The Liberator*.

Finally, family is very important to all of us. For me, this includes Victor Alonso, Miguel Alonso, Lucinda Alonso, Pablo Alonso, Lisa Koroleva, and Carolyn Beck. All read the story and discussed its plot and characters and got to know Martha and Jake almost as well as I did.

To all, I owe a great deal. But, mostly, for understanding Jake, I looked to my grandson, Joseph Alonso, to whom this book is dedicated.

HARRIET HYMAN ALONSO

To learn more about the facts behind the story, be sure to visit http://harrietalonso.com.

To reach the curriculum guide for this book, be sure to visit www.sevenstories.com.